BY MARGARET GUREVICH

Penguin Workshop

PENGUIN WORKSHOP
An imprint of Penguin Random House LLC, New York

First published in the United States of America by Penguin Workshop, an imprint of Penguin Random House LLC, New York, 2024

Text copyright © 2024 by Margaret Gurevich

Photo credits: ii–iii: (brick wall texture) Anzela Ksenofontova/iStock/Getty Images; 229: (composition book) SchulteProductions/iStock/Getty Images; 230–232: (lined paper) The_Pixle/iStock/Getty Images

Penguin supports copyright. Copyright fuels creativity, encourages diverse voices, promotes free speech, and creates a vibrant culture. Thank you for buying an authorized edition of this book and for complying with copyright laws by not reproducing, scanning, or distributing any part of it in any form without permission. You are supporting writers and allowing Penguin to continue to publish books for every reader.

PENGUIN is a registered trademark and PENGUIN WORKSHOP is a trademark of Penguin Books Ltd, and the W colophon is a registered trademark of Penguin Random House LLC.

Visit us online at penguinrandomhouse.com.

Library of Congress Cataloging-in-Publication Data is available.

Printed in the United States of America

ISBN 9780593659434

1st Printing

LSCC

Design by Mary Claire Cruz

This book is a work of fiction. Any references to historical events, real people, or real places are used fictitiously. Other names, characters, places, and events are products of the author's imagination, and any resemblance to actual events or places or persons, living or dead, is entirely coincidental.

The publisher does not have any control over and does not assume any responsibility for author or third-party websites or their content.

To Noah and Stu always—MG

CHAPTER 1

When people leave you, it's supposed to pour.

But the unusually hot November sun has other plans.

"Well," Dad says as he puts the last moving box into his trunk, "that's that." He shoves his hands into his pockets and forces a smile.

"That's that," I repeat, like it means something. Like he's just going away to perform in a comedy festival as he's done on other weekends. But that's not it at all. The next time he's here, it will be to pick me up. Not to come home.

"Sooo." He rocks back and forth on his heels. "I'll see you next weekend." He takes his hands out of his pockets and pulls me to him.

His breath catches as he hugs me tight, making the lump in my throat even bigger. My eyes water, and tears mingle with the dampness of his shirt. I pull away because I know Babushka is looking through the window, and she wouldn't approve.

Slozi goryu ne pomozhet, she always says. Tears won't help sorrow.

"It will be okay," I say. "We'll get through this." I've heard him and Mama say this, but the words sound wrong on my lips. Still, Dad nods, eyes distant.

He kisses the top of my hair. "Are you sure you're only in sixth grade?"

Babushka knocks on the window, and Dad gives me one last hug and jogs to his car.

I wait until the words #1COMIC are only dots on his New Jersey license plate before running inside. Until I'm certain my eyes are dry, and my lips don't tremble.

"The Russian Gourmet opens in half an hour," Babushka says as soon as I walk into our store's kitchen.

I know she and my dad didn't really get along, but I can't believe she's acting like this is a regular day.

At least Mama will be in my corner. There's no way *she's* up to working.

"Mama?" I say as she places sliced carrots on top of the gefilte fish.

She straightens her sagging shoulders. "Your grandma's right. The deli can't run itself."

"But—"

Babushka positions herself between Mama and me and drapes a hefty arm around each of our shoulders.

Mama's eyes are glassy, and she bites her lip.

"Let me tell you both something about the women in our family. We're strong. We can get through anything. Your great-grandma used to say," she pauses, kisses her fingertips, and raises them to the ceiling, "'*Slozi goryu*—'"

"'*Ne pomozhet*,'" I finish.

"That's right," she says, pulling me into her soft middle. Mama straightens her shoulders and adds fresh dill to the fish.

I blink back fresh tears.

"I guess I'll go shower," I say. My clothes feel extra sticky.

"Good girl," Babushka says. She glances at Mama. "Sarah, why don't you take a few minutes, too?"

Mama hugs me, and we trudge up the stairs that connect our two lives. Thunder rumbles in the distance. A few gray clouds try to sneak past the sun, but it pushes them away.

"Nice try," I whisper, but *slozi goryu ne pomozhet*.

Freshly showered, I inhale the smell of marinated pickles and fried onions as I place the brown cardboard box beside the magazine display in our store.

The magazine, *Otvet*—or *The Answer*—is like Russia's version of the *Enquirer*. This week's cover has a UFO on it, and side stories about talking dogs, celebrities, and Russians' favorite remedy for all diseases—fresh garlic.

My phone pings as I finish the last row. Val. Val has always been there for me, but she's been especially supportive since I told her in secret that my dad was leaving today. She even offered to let me hold on to her Moana Funko Pop! for good luck, which, coming from her, was a big deal.

> You okay?

Babushka is not looking in my direction, so I quickly type back.

> Russians don't cry, so I guess so.

> Just keep swimming.

She adds a picture of Dory from *Finding Nemo*. I laugh, then quickly pocket my phone when Babushka glares at me.

Time for the mahtroshka display.

The Russian Gourmet is a Russian grocery store and deli, but we also sell Russian books, magazines, and toys. Mahtroshkas are dolls within a doll. We have traditional ones that are painted to look like old Russian grandmas with kerchiefs around their heads, but we also have modern ones, like the Simpsons. You open up Homer to reveal a smaller Marge and keep opening until you have a tiny Maggie.

Usually, Dad helps me arrange the mahtroshkas, and we make up stories about them. For example, instead of keeping Snoopy near Charlie Brown, we put him next to Scooby-Doo, because his Red Baron adventures would fit right in with the Scooby gang. It's already weird working without him today. Not for Baba, though. She always complains that he needs to help more and talk less. She also never liked our creative mahtroshka maneuvers. But the part that bugged her most was when Dad would zone out and craft stand-up routines in his head.

I do that, too. It helps me pass the time and ignore the rude comments. Not to say I don't like working here. It's been fun being here with Dad, Mama, and Baba, all of us banding together to make this store great. I started helping last year—just a few hours a week—and the customers quickly learned I knew my stuff and could pack things up just as quickly as Mama and Baba, so it made me feel grown-up and important. But the mental stand-up routines come in handy for the handful of obnoxious customers. Plus, I'm better at faking interest in their stories than Dad, so Baba doesn't get annoyed with me.

"Maya," Babushka says, "we're opening in five."

I move Elsa beside Rudolph, put on my gloves and hairnet, and brace myself for the line that's formed outside. Mama winks at me and does the same.

"Was that Val? You didn't say anything to her, did you?"

Mama doesn't like me to share family business. "She's my best friend."

She frowns but kisses my forehead. "Here we go," she says under her breath. "Judgy Russian ladies at twelve o'clock."

I laugh as Babushka flips the Closed sign to Open. "*Zahoditze, zahoditze,*" she says, welcoming everyone inside.

People shove each other, trying to grab numbers, and I'm glad I have the counter for protection. The three of us divide and conquer. I get lucky with Mrs. Sanchez.

She uses a cane to push her skinny eighty-five-year-old body to the counter. Sometimes, I think the cane is just for show—or to whack people in line.

"What can I get for you today?" I ask. Mrs. Sanchez is loud and bossy, and I admire that. I love customers' surprised faces when they realize she won't let anyone push her around. I also love her lavender hair.

"What's fresh today?"

I resist the urge to roll my eyes. "It's all fresh *every* day."

"Hmph," she says, like she doesn't believe me. It's the same conversation we have each time she comes.

I lean forward, like I'm going to tell her a secret. "Just to show you how sure I am, I'll throw in an extra pirozhok for free." This is part of our routine, too. Good thing she buys a lot, or we'd go broke. The pirozhki, dough stuffed with chicken, beef, or veggies, are our best sellers.

A look of triumph crosses her face. "Deal. I'll also have the herring salad, poppy seed cake, and those Russian ravioli, what are they called again?"

"Pelmeni." I pack her items, moving her along.

She nods. "Yes, those. I don't miss my dieting days, I'll tell you that." She slaps a bony hip and laughs.

"Why diet when you can eat?" I wink at her and bring her food to the register.

"You're a smart girl." She places a quarter in the tip jar as the line grows. "And funny, just like your dad."

I force a smile. "He's performing later. That's why he's not here." Like she even asked.

Mrs. Sanchez nods and pats my hand. "Good for him." I'll have to change my gloves now, but I appreciate her kindness.

Baba motions Mrs. Sanchez to the cash register, and I quickly change my gloves. I cringe when I see my next customer.

"Good morning," Mrs. Nelson says. Her daughter Lacey is in my sixth-grade class at McKinley Elementary. When I met Lacey in kindergarten, her last name was Katznelson, but by second grade, it was just Nelson. The Katz in front of it made it "too Russian," according to her mom. I wonder if she knows that Lacey talks in Russian whenever she wants someone to feel left out. Maybe that was the compromise: Being "other" is okay as long as you make those around you feel less than.

"How can I help you today?" The hot-hot-hot starts in my stomach. My fingers tingle inside the gloves, like the tiny needles people get when their feet fall asleep. I try to shake it off. Mrs. Nelson notices everything, and I don't need her going home and telling Lacey I was being weird.

"To be honest," she says, unbuttoning her leather jacket, "none of this stuff compares to my mother's home cooking. God rest her soul." Her eyes flitter to the ceiling lights. "But beggars can't be choosers, right?"

I grit my teeth and hope it looks like a toothy smile. "Well, uh, thanks for choosing us." *Next time, please choose someone else.*

She fans herself. "Have you thought about turning on the air?"

"In November?"

She purses her lips. "It may be November outside, but it's June in here. And with this line," she waves her hand in the air, "people will start passing out."

I can't help myself. "Have you seen this month's *Otvet*? Garlic cures all. Can I interest you in our delicious cheesy garlic spread?"

Mrs. Nelson peers into the glass display case, staring extra hard at the thermometer. Like we would risk poisoning the town! "Fine. I'll take a pound."

I scoop a generous helping into our one-pound container and set it on the scale. Perfect. "What else?"

Her eyes zero in on my gloves. "Are those clean, dear?"

I pretend I'm my dad onstage. "Yup. I changed them right before I used the bathroom."

Mrs. Nelson's lips pucker. "That better be a joke."

Baba is within earshot, and her eye is twitching. I sigh. "It is. I changed them right after I helped Mrs. Sanchez."

"It's not personal," she says in a voice dripping with sugar substitute. "I just know how kids can be."

"Yes, of course." Except . . . she always asks Mama and Babushka the same thing when they wait on her.

"Will there be anything else?" Widest smile ever.

She taps her fingers on the glass case, even though there's a sign asking people not to do that. Fingerprints are a pain to clean off. "Throw in four pirozhki, a pound of pelmeni, a large container of borscht, the gefilte fish, aaaand . . ." More tapping on the case.

"How about our shashlik? Everyone loves the shish kabob."

She shrugs. "That's fine. Whatever you think is best." She leans in as I quickly pack up her food. If she's worried about germ-spreading, she shouldn't be so close. "I saw your dad's packed car when I was out for my morning jog. Big comedy trip?"

My hand slips, and the container with the pirozhki falls behind the counter.

A loud laugh bursts from her lips. "I won't be taking those."

"I'll be right back." I rip off the gloves and run into the bathroom to wash my hands. Lots of handwashing and cold air don't mix. The combo makes my hands extra dry, and changing gloves feels like sandpaper on my skin. I take a deep breath and return to Mrs. Nelson, making sure she's watching when I put on a new pair of gloves and pack fresh pirozhki.

Mrs. Nelson purses her lips. "Have a good day, Maya. And give your dad my best."

"You can tell him yourself when he gets back." The words just slip out.

Mrs. Nelson smirks. "Will do."

It seems she doesn't believe he'll be back. I don't know if *I* believe it either, but I *need* to. And why wouldn't he? Mama and Dad called this a "separation," not a "divorce." Sure, they both have big lawyers, but apparently you need that to work stuff out—like who gets to see me when—even when you're just separated.

"Maya," Mama had said when she and Dad sat me down one month ago, "we want to make this as easy on you as possible." We were on our blue fabric couch—the one Dad got with his bargaining skills at a Black Friday sale the year before. They were on either side of me, and they looked at each other over my head, and then each took one of my hands. Dad was still living with us, but they had apparently already started the separation talks months before. I hadn't known that until that moment.

"Just because your mom and I are going through something tough right now doesn't mean we can't try to make things smoother for you," Dad added, squeezing my hand.

I just nodded because "smoother" would have meant keeping everything the same. "Smoother" would have been no lawyers, no sharing weekends, and Dad not getting an apartment in New York. I focused on Dad's words *right now*. That made it sound like this was temporary. Like once they went through whatever this was, all would be better. This wasn't a period. It was a comma—one big run-on sentence where things weren't over.

Mama takes the next customer, but her gaze follows Mrs. Nelson's stroll to the cash register. My hands tingle beneath my gloves, and the hot-hot-hot spreads to my arms. I look at the big line ahead of me and try to ignore Mrs. Nelson's swagger. I imagine her as a mahtroshka doll—getting smaller and smaller, until she's so tiny, what she thinks doesn't matter at all.

CHAPTER 2

Two days later, Val spreads the contents of her lunch on the cafeteria table and waves her toasted banana-Nutella sandwich in the air. "Swap?" she asks.

"Your grandma won't mind?"

Val grins. "Please. She packs me two *hoping* I'll give one to you. The catch," she winks at me, "is that you have to tell her how much you loved it the next time you see her."

"As long as you praise Babushka's pirozhok, too," I add.

She laughs. "Deal."

I unwrap both of my perfectly browned pastries. "Do you want the one with meat or the one with mashed potato?"

Val chooses the mashed potato filling. Then, she counts to three, and we bite into our trades at the same time. Lacey Nelson and Kat Antonov are sitting a few seats down from us, giggling. Every few seconds, they glance in our direction and say something in Russian, loud enough for me to hear. I catch only a few words. I can understand Russian well if people speak slowly. Kat and Lacey speak in turbo speed on purpose.

They scoot closer to us. "You guys want to play elastics at recess?" Lacey asks. Her pink, glittery lip gloss sparkles under the fluorescent cafeteria lights.

Val raises her eyebrows. We don't love playing with them because the rules always change, but we do like the game. And playing might help take my mind off my dad. I shrug. "Why not?"

The lunch aide dismisses our table, and Lacey grabs Kat's hand, who grabs mine, and I grab Val's. Kat and Lacey look at each other, smirk, and say, *"Bistreya, bistreya,"* in unison as they pull us with them.

Val rolls her eyes. She's heard them say that often enough to know what it means. But we don't go faster, faster. I disentangle my hand from Kat's and let her and Lacey run ahead.

"You know they're going to make us hold the rope, right?" Val says when they're out of earshot.

I bite my lip and nod.

"You sure you want to play?" She stops walking and puts her hand on my shoulder. "We can still back out. No big deal."

If we back out, then it becomes a big deal. They'll ask why and pout, and if I say I changed my mind, I'll sound lame.

"I'll be fine."

I hope I will. Val knows about the hot-hot-hot feeling I get, and the random things that trigger it sometimes—like elastics. But even she doesn't know how quickly it happens or how big it can get. She knows some things—like germs—make me nervous. She doesn't think I'm weird, because mice make *her* nervous. So, she thinks it's the same, and that I'm just like her—but it's not, and sometimes I feel like I'm not. I'm not like anyone.

Val squints her eyes and gets super close to my face. She wrinkles her nose. "My sixth sense tells me you're telling the truth."

I laugh. Sure enough, when we get to Kat and Lacey, they toss me the elastic—similar to a giant rubber band—and it encircles our little group. Val and I place it around our ankles and then move to opposite corners, stretching the band out. At least I'm wearing leggings today. This would be much worse if it was warm enough for shorts and the rope was touching my skin.

Lacey jumps inside the stretched-out rectangle as the four of us shout "In!"

"Out!" we shout again as her ankles rest along each side of the rope.

"Side by side!" Lacey jumps from one side of the elastic to the other.

"In, out, on!" She lands with a sneaker on top of each rope piece.

"My turn!" Kat shouts.

Val makes a silly face at me and sticks out her tongue. I do the same, my body relaxing.

But as both Kat and Lacey finish the ankle level, I feel the hot-hot-hot coming. Knees level, where the rope is pulled even tighter against the legs, is next. I picture Lacey and Kat's feet flying through the air and landing with a triumphant thud on the elastic, the rope slicing across my leggings.

I peek at the clock by the school's entrance. "You guys," I say. "There's only five minutes left. I think we should pack up." My voice is shaky. I can't tell if Kat and Lacey notice, but Val does.

"Uh, yeah. It's almost time," Val chimes in. Her face looks worried. I hate that I worry her. She has enough to stress about. She and her eight-year-old brother, Joey, live with their grandparents, who are absolutely the sweetest, but lately, they've been too nervous to drive or leave the house much. They've been ordering everything they need online, and in a pinch, they'll walk to the grocery store a mile away, splitting grocery bags between the four of them on the way home. Val says she doesn't mind it—she says she feels like Belle going to the market in *Beauty and the Beast*—but I know she's on edge about how they're doing.

"We have plenty of time for knees." Lacey tosses her hair. Her lip gloss shines brighter.

I'll be fine, I tell myself. The three of them stare at me. Val starts getting out of the rope. "C'mon," Lacey whines. "Why are you being weird?"

The hot-hot-hot creeps up my calves. My palms get sweaty. Kat and Lacey are rolling their eyes at each other. I don't want to be *weird*.

I move the rope to my knees, and Val gives me a questioning look as she drags the rope up her legs. She pauses at her shins, and she waits for my okay. I nod, and she slowly raises the rope to her knees.

In, out, side by side, in, out . . . I shut my eyes as Lacey jumps on the elastic with all her might. The rope presses into my leggings. Too tight.

I read that when you have cuts, germs can get inside them in school. Regular, little cuts. One day, you're fine, sitting at your desk, working on a math problem. The next day, something in the air, someone's sweat or other ickiness, seeps into that cut and it's inflamed and red and oozing.

The bell rings—a few seconds too late. My heart beats quickly. My brain tells me there's a cut sliced into my skin from the elastics. I'm sure of it.

The lunch aide instructs everyone to file in, and I make a beeline to the front of the line and ask to use the bathroom. Inside the stall, I scan my knees and ankles for rope scrapes. I breathe a sigh of relief at the unmarked space behind my knees, but as I pull my leggings back up, I see it. A small rope burn by my ankle. Why didn't I feel it? The skin isn't broken, but the hot-hot-hot starts anyway—like I knew it would. I can't stop it. My stomach clenches, and my head feels full, like someone stuffed it with cotton. Tingles start at my toes, and my body feels hot—like that feeling you get when you realize everyone is staring at you because you've had spinach stuck between your front teeth all day. I shake my hands to get the tingles out and close my eyes.

I always worried about things, but when it started to get worse a few months ago, I realized repeating stuff in my head helps lessen the hot-hot-hot and tingles because I just focus on the phrases and not on how I'm feeling. *In, out, side by side, in, out, on. In, out, side by side, in, out, on.* As I walk back to class, I repeat the words to myself to block out the worry. At my locker, I pull my sock up over the red line and my leggings down over my sock. Germs can't seep through two layers, can they? *In, out, side by side, in, out, on. In, out, side by side, in, out, on.*

All okay? Val mouths when I sit down at my desk.

I feel my leggings ride up, but I give her a thumbs-up and look for a new pattern to focus on. I neatly stack my rainbow-colored pencils on my desk. Each pencil point is sharpened to the same height. Barry Baker's fingers, still sticky from whatever he was eating at lunch, inch closer to my desk. I rub my sweaty palms on my leggings, and he quickly snags a shimmery red pencil.

Saliva pools in my mouth, and my breath comes in fast bursts. Without thinking, I grab the pencil out of his hand, and the stickiness transfers to my skin.

"Ow! I was just looking at them." His hand shoots high in the air, and he doesn't wait for Ms. Banta to call on him. "Maya grabbed her pencils and hurt my fingers."

Ms. Banta cocks her head to the side and looks at us. "She grabbed her *own* pencils? How did that hurt *your* fingers?"

"Never mind," Barry mumbles.

"Do you want to see Ms. Graham?" Ms. Banta's voice is always so calm and soothing, just like her outfits. Today, she's wearing a navy blouse, black skirt, and navy heels. Her shoes always match her top. I like the matchiness.

Barry scowls. "I said never mind. I don't need the nurse."

In, out, side by side, in, out, on.

I use my non-sticky hand to rearrange the pencils and try to focus on Ms. Banta's geography lesson. My eyes zero in on the big map she attaches to the board. I look at the stretches of land and water and squint to see each tiny letter. Anything to stop thinking about the hot-hot-hot slowly creeping up my arms and legs.

CHAPTER 3

On Saturday, Babushka and Mama sit on the couch and wring their hands. Their eyes dart from the television to the clock on the wall to Mama's cell phone. One, two, three. One, two, three. It's a familiar pattern, their eyes checking all the clocks as if one display will be different from another. I call it the *Waiting for Dad Waltz*.

Dad's "on time" is twenty-five to thirty minutes late. Mama once read an article suggesting the "chronically late" be told to arrive somewhere thirty minutes ahead of schedule. Dad saw right through this, and his pattern stayed the same.

"*Kazhdi raz,*" Babushka murmurs.

"Exactly," I say, "*every time.* So, why are you worried?"

She opens her mouth to say something, shakes her head, and walks into the kitchen. From what I understand, Babushka always had reservations about my dad. Well . . . maybe not in the beginning, but once his passion for the law was replaced with his passion for comedy, things went downhill quick.

I look at the clock. 4:22. He was supposed to be here at 4:00. That would have been early, based on Dad Time. Especially now that he's in New York and has to navigate a bridge and a tunnel.

Mama smooths her hands over her flowery skirt and tucks her hair behind her ears.

"How hard is it to text?" she asks, picking up her phone and throwing it back down on the couch.

4:27.

"I bet he'll be here in three minutes," I say, sitting beside her.

"I just don't want you to be disappointed." She strokes my hair and sighs. "It's your first time together since . . . I just didn't want him to be late."

It won't help to point out that he's only late to the outside world. "I know he's coming." I smile at her and wrinkle my nose. She wrinkles her nose, too, and smiles back, lightening the weight on my shoulders. When Mama worries, I do, too.

4:29, and the doorbell rings.

"*Slava bogu!*" Babushka's yell of relief filters in from the kitchen.

I give Mama an I-told-you-so look and fling open the door.

"Tunnel traffic was a bear," Dad says. "I'm sorry I'm late."

He's wearing his blue-and-white checkered flannel shirt—my favorite. I wrap my arms around him and bury my face in the shirt's softness. "You're on time for you."

He kisses the top of my hair. "You always get me." I hear the grin in his voice.

"Unlike me?" Mama says.

I pull away and peek at her face. She's smiling a tight smile, the kind she wears when she wants to look like she's kidding, but I know she's annoyed.

"Sarah." He draws out her name, so it sounds like it has four syllables.

"I'm sorry," she mumbles. "Now's not the time." She jerks her head slightly in my direction, and Dad nods.

I look from one to the other. Dad's right eyebrow twitches. Mama's smile trembles. They're both trying so hard to be . . . *nice* . . . and I hate it, because it's not a real *nice* but an act. For me.

I bite the inside of my cheek. "What's the plan for tonight?"

Dad's bounce returns. He's becoming real again and not the fake *nice* guy from seconds ago. "New restaurant in the Village you'll love and then some city exploring."

I love my dad's New York. He knows all the tiny, out-there haunts. When we visited as a family, we never did touristy things. It always felt like the city revolved around *us*.

Babushka comes back into the living room. "James." She wipes her hand on her apron and extends it to Dad.

He shakes it firmly. "Good to see you, Clara."

She snorts. "I bet."

A deep sigh rises from her belly, through her chest, out her mouth, into the room. It's sad and worried and surrounds us.

I wrap my arms around her because I know that's what she needs. "I'll miss you."

She pulls me close to her. "You too, *Zaichik.*" Her name for me since before I can remember: her bunny.

Mama hugs me tightly, too.

"It's just a weekend," I tell her, hugging her back.

She nods, but her eyes tear up. "Maya can't go to your spots, James," she says over my head.

She's talking about spots at comedy clubs, where Dad gets to perform short sets of his stand-up material. I wince; these sets are the only way Dad can get on a manager's radar.

With a manager, Dad could get better-paying gigs and spots at normal hours. He wouldn't have to chase late-night stage time. A week before he moved out, he and Mama had a big fight because he was asked to fill in for a 2:00 a.m. cancellation. Some big biz manager was going to be there, and Dad said this could be "IT."

So he thought that was his chance. But he was out super late the night before, and the night before that, and Mama didn't want him to go. He went anyway. And the manager didn't even show.

Mama crosses her arms over her chest. "I mean it, James."

Dad's jaw tenses. "Got it," he says.

I want to tell her that being seen is the answer to their problems. Once Dad gets a manager and makes it big, he can be around more, and there won't be anything to fight about. He could come back home.

But I know this isn't the time. Dad clenches his jaw again, and Mama nervously taps her foot. They whisper something to each other, and then Dad closes the door behind us.

CHAPTER 4

"You're looking very cosmopolitan, kid," Dad says as he looks behind him and eases onto the highway. "Love the brown ankle boots."

I beam. The thing with going to New York City is that you have to look stylish but not I'm-going-to-the-ball fancy. Mama doesn't let me wear makeup, but she's okay with fruity lip balms, so I'm wearing my favorite flavor, Raspberry Punch. I pull down the visor and smack my lips together, like I've seen Kat and Lacey do.

"Thanks. I was trying to get the right blend of chic."

Dad laughs. "Nothing says chic like leopard print leggings."

This is one of the many reasons I love my dad. He notices stuff like leggings and boots. When he and Mama were together, she'd always say she struck gold because he was one of the only husbands she knew who noticed the little things, like her hair parted in a different direction. Lately, I've been wondering when that sparkle became fool's gold and it stopped being enough.

"What do you think?" Dad asks as we walk into Brody's.

The fireplace near the entrance casts a soft glow on the mahogany walls. The other thing I notice is that the silverware is resting on napkins, rather than directly on the tables. I hate when restaurants place the silverware right on the table that too many fingers touched before mine.

My dad seems to think my silence means I hate it. "If this place isn't for you," he says, "we can go somewhere else. I just thought I remembered you saying you wanted to try more vegan stuff, and—"

Just like his happiness, his nervous energy can be contagious, too. I have enough of my own nervousness. I place my hand on his arm. "Brody's is great!"

He raises an eyebrow.

"Really." I reassure him by following the directions on the sign in front of us and choosing a table.

Honestly? I was sold at the silverware on the napkins. The fact that it's vegan just sweetens the deal. Meat ups the hot-hot-hot. It's hard for me to look at a piece of chicken and not wonder if it's been cooked enough. I've read a lot about people getting sick from raw chicken. Then, there was mad cow disease years ago with beef. I stumbled upon that little fact during a social studies lesson, and now I can't eat beef without wondering if it's contaminated. Vegan food is easier. No one ever died from undercooked broccoli.

I haven't told him any of this, though. I don't know where I'd start. He and Mama don't know about the hot-hot-hot. And it doesn't seem right to tell either of them now when they have enough to think about.

"My lady." Dad bows as he pulls out my chair.

"Why thank you, sir," I say in a very bad British accent. I take an extra napkin and lay it across my lap.

"It's nice not having to cook, right?" Dad asks.

It is, and it isn't. At least I know how The Russian Gourmet food is prepared. But he looks so eager. "Sure is."

"I've missed the store," he says.

"Really?" Even before he moved out, he worked at the store less and less. "But you never seemed to like it."

Dad plays with the salt and pepper shakers on the table. "I liked it fine." He doesn't sound convincing.

But you like comedy more. Baba's words flash in my head like a neon hotel sign.

Two months before he moved out, Dad was in the city passing out flyers for a comedy show. If enough people came to the show with his flyer, he'd be able to perform in the show, too.

Mama and Baba were having their usual argument about Dad not helping enough at the deli. And, as usual, I was eavesdropping instead of getting ready for bed.

"No, Mama," my mom had said, "he doesn't hate the store."

"Please, Sarah, just admit he doesn't like it here."

"Comedy is his dream," Mama said.

Baba sighed. "And the store is yours."

"Can't we have two dreams? We're two people, after all," Mama said, her voice sad and tired. *Yes!* I thought. It's like when Mama wanted to watch *Halloween Terror* and Dad wanted an artsy flick. They settled on a foreign horror movie about a killer poet. It's just about compromise.

"If he were willing to sacrifice for you, like you are for him, it might work. But, right now, you're here, and he's all the way here." I imagined her holding her arms so far apart there was no way of joining them in the middle. I heard Baba walking, probably toward Mama. "So, at the least . . ." her voice was kinder now, softer, "you need to acknowledge that comedy is more important to him."

That was enough for me, and I crept back upstairs.

I wondered if Baba meant that comedy was more important to him than his family.

"Maya," Dad says now, putting his hand on mine.

"Hmm?"

He suddenly looks sad. "The best part about the store was being there with you and Mama." Baba was wrong. Comedy is *not* more important to him than we are. It's just more important than the store. But to Baba it's all the same.

"You can make a guest appearance anytime," I say gently.

He could do spots at our store just like he does at the clubs. *Appearing two afternoons this week, Jaaaames Greenspan! Get your olivyeh salad with a side of shtick.*

He laughs. "I don't think Babushka would love that."

Or maybe she would? If she saw he was trying and *sacrificing*, those arms could meet in the middle after all.

"Did I hear something about appearances?" our waiter interrupts. Todd, according to his name tag, has a joke-a-second personality that screams comic, but I don't understand most of his act.

He twirls an invisible mustache and wiggles his eyebrows. "Is the lady an aspiring comedian, too?"

I make a huge X with my arms. Dozens of people staring at me under a hot spotlight seems as fun as eating with rusty utensils.

Dad winks at me. "Maya has skills."

Todd laughs. "If they are anything like her cooking skills, I think I'm safe."

My gut rumbles, and not for food. What is he talking about? Dad's face reddens.

"Todd, I think we're ready to order." He doesn't look at me. My palms start to sweat, and the backs of my knees throb. My stomach clenches, and my mouth twitches.

"Sure thing," Todd says, clearly clueless that anything is off. "I gotta warn you, though . . ." He turns to me. "We don't serve any of that weird Russian gelatin or hot dog salad here."

I look from Dad to Todd, and it clicks. He's been making fun of our store in his bits.

Suddenly, Baba's thoughts about all of it being connected make total sense. If he doesn't like the store and what we do there, if he'd go as far as making *fun* of the food we sell . . . Maybe comedy *is* more important than we are. Cotton fills my head, and a rushing sound starts in my ears. I need to get out of here. "Bathroom."

Dad places his hand on my shoulder, and I shake him off and bolt toward the unisex stick figures at the back of the restaurant.

Fortunately, the room is clean, and the garbage is not overflowing. *You'll be fine*, I tell myself as I stare into the mirror. I run cold water onto a paper towel and gently wipe my face.

You'll be fine, I tell myself again, closing my eyes. I remember a unit we did in health class on calming the mind. I take a deep breath in through my nose and let it out slowly through my mouth. I do this four times. Then, once more for good luck. When I open my eyes, I'm better. No twitching, no sweaty palms, no throbbing knees. The rushing sound in my head, while not totally gone, is a distant, low hum. I wash my hands and use the edge of my sleeve to open the door.

"I ordered for you," Dad says, moving his fork from one hand to the other. "I hope that's okay."

I shrug. "As long as there's nothing disgusting and Russian, we're good."

Dad leans in and moves a strand of hair from my eyes. "We were just workshopping our material the other night. Todd took things out of context."

"So you're not making fun of our life in your bits?"

Dad plays with his fork, dragging it across his napkin, shredding the white paper. "It's my life, too. I can't have an opinion on congealed fat?" He smiles.

I rip my napkin into strips, too. We used to make fun of the cholodetz together, but it's different now. "It's not—" I'm about to say that it's not his life anymore, but that thought makes my fingers tingle. I backtrack. "It's just weird, that's all."

He nods and puts his hand on mine. I notice he's still wearing his wedding ring. That *has* to be a good thing. "I never say anything about you and Mama. The store, though?" He shrugs. "Laughing about all that makes everything . . ." He pauses and shreds more of his napkin.

He looks sad again. "Laughing makes it easier," I say.

"Yeah. Laughing is good." He squeezes my hand.

Todd brings our food, and Dad waves him away when he pulls out a notepad to share his latest jokes.

"You know what they say in the comedy world?" Dad says, digging into his "sweet & sour chikin." "'Comedy equals tragedy plus time.'" He winks at me.

The sauce from the teriyaki eggplant pools in the corner of my plate. "You thought working at the store was a tragedy?"

Dad rolls his eyes. "I mean in general. Take anything that's tough in the moment, give it time, and one day you can—hopefully—find humor in the hardest situations."

I nod. "I mean, if you can't laugh at pieces of meat stuck in jelled fat drippings, what can you laugh at?"

His eyes brighten. "Not at the hot dog salad mixed with peas, that's for sure."

"Never! That's a staple!" The tingling has stopped, and we're both laughing now.

Dad's dimple comes out in full force. He raises his fork in the air like a toast. "Like I said, you get me."

At 9:15, we're standing in front of the Comic Nook.

Mama and I came here a few times with Dad to pick up checks. Having seen comedians on TV, I'd expected a larger-than-life place lit up in lights with columns in the front. I'd expected some host, dressed to the nines, greeting us at the door and ushering Dad in like he was famous. But the building isn't fancy at all. The outside is made up of faded red bricks and peeling red paint. The words *Comic Nook* are surrounded by those little lights actors have around their dressing room mirrors, but they're not lit up or flashing. In the beginning, I was disappointed by that.

But the second I saw how happy the Nook made my dad, how his face glowed at the entrance as if *it* were surrounded by lights, I was hooked, too.

And fancy places don't have Celeste, who is better than any bouncer.

"Hey, sugar," she says, when Dad and I walk into the club. Her salt-and-pepper hair is accented with cotton-candy-blue bangs, and she's wearing a leopard print full-body leotard with black stiletto heels.

"Hiya," I say. I unzip my coat so she can see my leopard print leggings.

"A girl after my own heart." She pulls me in for a hug and kisses my cheek with her sparkly, burgundy-painted lips.

My dad bounces from one foot to the other. "Who's in there today?" he asks, scanning the crowd through the club's open doors.

"I hear," Celeste whispers, "Artie Munch is making his rounds."

Dad's head whips toward her. "Now?"

She glances at her phone. "Should be."

"Who's Artie Munch?" I keep my voice low, just like Celeste.

"Only one of the best managers in the city," Dad says. He runs his hand through his hair and furrows his brows.

My heart beats quickly. This is his chance. "You *have* to do a spot!"

Celeste opens a notebook and scans the names on the list. "I can fit you in, James."

Dad's face lights up and, just as quickly, the bulb burns out. "I can't."

Celeste snorts. "Of course you can! Don't start that 'I'm not good enough' nonsense."

He looks at me and shakes his head. "I promised your mom . . ."

"I can stay in the lobby with Celeste. I won't go inside," I promise, giving him my biggest smile.

I think back to the last fight my parents had before he moved out. Dad performing while he's with me might annoy Mama at first, but when he gets his big break, it will all be worth it.

Dad looks from me to Celeste and back to me.

"It's your call," Celeste says, "but she's safe with me, if that's what you're worried about."

I grab his arm. "Please, Dad. You gotta."

He pauses for one more second before he winks at me. "If I gotta, then I gotta, right?"

Celeste texts something into her phone, and two minutes later, we hear "James Greenspan" echo from inside the club.

He and Celeste do a fist bump, then splay their fingers like the fists are exploding. *"Kapow!"* they say at the same time, and he jogs out to the stage.

"What was *that*?" I ask.

Celeste laughs. "We did that on a whim the first time he performed here, and now it's a thing. Won't go onstage without *kapowing* someone first."

It's like getting the code to some highly classified mission; witnessing that *kapow* makes me want to see his act even more. I give Celeste a pleading look, hoping she'll take pity on me.

She grins. "We'll stand all the way in the back, and I'll chaperone."

A rush of energy zaps through me at the secrecy and finally being inside a club and seeing my dad's secret world; I love being one of many in this tiny space. The spotlight shines on my dad, and he runs onto the stage and grabs the mic.

He tosses it in the air and does a quick spin before catching it. The audience applauds.

Dad bows. "Thank you very much. That's my time." Then, he pretends to walk off the stage.

The crowd chuckles, and that's all Dad needs. His body leans in toward the audience, and I feel the electricity. It's like he's talking to everyone and just to you at the same time.

"So," he says, "I'm Russian." There are some hollers from the audience.

"Yeah, thanks. I mean, it's not my doing, but okay." He pauses and takes a sip of water. "I'll tell you what I did do, though. I worked in a Russian deli. And the requests we got there? Oh boy!"

He launches into the time Mrs. Nelson wanted us to change the coloring of the beet salad. To green. It was St. Paddy's Day, after all.

"He's killing it tonight," Celeste says between chortles.

"Definitely," I say as he begins a bit about the time he worked as a tour guide during college. He'd find a way to stay in the cafeteria and get free samples all day! *Have you ever seen such detail in a pizza pan? Let's all take a closer look.*

And then it's over, and Dad is running up to me, big smile on his face, cheers echoing around him. He grabs me by the waist, carries me back into the lobby, and spins me around.

"We killed it!" he says.

I laugh. "We did!" *I* helped make this happen!

"This could be it, honey!" he says in an excited but hushed voice. "I saw Artie. Front row. Laughing at everything!"

"You're the man, James," Celeste says. "I'll be sure to quiz him when he comes out."

We step out of the club onto MacDougal Street and start walking to his apartment. It's late, but I don't want the night to end.

"Here's a question for you," he says as if reading my mind. "Turning left will put us near ice cream; right will be my place. What say you?"

It's after ten, and I know Mama would be mad if she knew. I feel bad because we already lied to her tonight—even if she never finds out. Still, I put my finger to my lips, duck into a nearly empty convenience store, and call her to say good night. Then, I take my dad's hand and we turn left.

CHAPTER 5

Monday is an up-up-up day. Mama and Babushka are busy setting up the store, so I grab a banana and homemade apple muffin and run out the door. I'm not even at the end of my block before Val tugs on my backpack.

"Heya, Mayannaise!" she sings. I guess it's a good Monday for her, too.

I tap my lips, trying to think of a silly way to say her name back.

"You're taking forever," she says, laughing. "How about ValPal?"

I wrinkle my nose. "I want to think of my own."

Val pretends to stifle a yawn. "Take your time."

I snap my fingers. "Got it. Valentine."

"Not bad," she says, impressed. "I feel so loooved."

I laugh and hike my backpack higher on my shoulders while Val wheels hers.

"Joey, my grandparents, and I walked to the new comic book store this weekend."

I know Val's little brother has been dying to get new Pokémon cards, and Val wanted a Disney pin she saw in the window. I also know the store is well over a mile from her house. "How are your legs?"

Val shrugs. "I'm tough. Besides, Gram and Gramps are way older than me, so if they can do it, so can Joey and I." She flexes her muscles. "How was your dad's?"

"I saw his comedy act," I whisper. "Like in an actual *comedy club*."

Val stops on the concrete. Her toe touches the crack in the middle of the sidewalk, and I try not to look at it. *Crack= bad luck. Crack=bad luck. Stop! Think comedy, comedy, comedy.*

Val squeezes my arm. "So? Tell me! Was it super glam and adult?"

I tell her about the spotlight on my dad and lurking in the back with Celeste. If Val had been there, she would have ignored all the rules and found a seat front and center. Heck, she'd have run up to the mic and done a bit herself.

"I'd be ah-may-zing onstage," she says, echoing my thoughts. "Can't you just see my name in lights? Do you think they have pink lights? How cool would that be?"

She continues talking about her future entertainment career. The fans, the lights, her sparkly shoes, and outfits.

"Ugh," she says as we round the corner to McKinley. "Barry's here already."

This would be a problem any other day, but today there's no knot in my stomach. I picture my dad onstage and grab an imaginary mic as a bit about Barry takes form. "Let's hear it for Maya Greenspan, ladies and gentlemen."

Val stops and laughs. "What are you doing?"

"My dad's act inspired me." I toss my imaginary mic in the air and motion for Val to keep walking.

"*So this kid in my class,*" I begin softly, "*keeps stashing my pencils. Has anyone checked the tree by his house? I bet he's squirreling them away for winter!*"

Val giggles and elbows me in the ribs. "Your dad's got competition."

The bell rings, and we push our way through the crowd.

"Good morning, everyone," Ms. Banta chirps when we reach our lockers. "Coats and backpacks away and check the board for today's plan."

Some kids were worried about getting Ms. Banta this year. There were rumors she was strict, but she just likes rules and order. That's probably why she's my favorite teacher. There are no grays in her class, and that makes me feel safe. I've had teachers who were super sweet, but their go-with-the-flow attitude sent my panic skyrocketing. Sometimes they'd change the daily routine "just to mix things up."

The Unexpected is the worst thing that can happen on hot-hot-hot days.

Ms. Banta writes the full schedule on the board each morning. She tries to keep it consistent, but it's not always possible. Like today.

My stomach gets rumbly when I see "Talent Show" in the number one spot of the day always reserved for math.

"Finally," Barry says, "something different."

An excited buzz fills the classroom.

Tingles start at my toes, and I organize my pencils in rainbow order.

"Why do you always do that?" Barry asks.

Red, orange, yellow, green, blue. "Do what?"

"Line your pencils up perfectly. It's kind of annoying." He takes out his own pencils, all yellow No. 2s, and places one at the top of his desk. It starts to roll down, and he makes a game of blowing at it so it reverses course before it reaches the edge. *Roll, roll, roll, phht. Roll, roll, roll, phht.* Spittle flies out of his mouth, and I move my chair away. He smirks and blows harder. The tingles rise to my ankles. How did an up-up-up morning change so quickly?

Val runs to my desk. "That's awesome, right?" she asks, pointing to the words *Talent Show*, which seem to have grown in size.

Awesome? No. Unexpected? Definitely. My stomach clenches. I clutch my pencils and focus on Val's wide eyes and waving hands.

"We can do an act together! I'll even let you put your name first," she says, bouncing on her toes.

"How about you leave my name totally out of it?" I do *not* need to get up in front of all those people.

Before Val can protest, Ms. Banta raises two fingers in the air—her signal for silence—and Val runs back to her seat.

"The cat's out of the bag," Ms. Banta says, pointing to the board. "We were supposed to tell you about the show later in the week, but I was told—oh, twenty minutes ago—to make the announcement today." She smiles tightly and adjusts the collar of her black silk blouse. Then, she runs her hands over her blue skirt. I zoom in on the motions and sit straighter in my chair. Seems like Ms. Banta doesn't like surprises either.

"As you know, the sixth graders participate in something special each year and present it to the whole school. Last year it was a game show."

The game show was pretty cool, especially when one of the contestants accidentally blurted out an inappropriate word instead of the right answer.

"This year," Ms. Banta continues, "the PTA committee decided on a sixth-grade talent show. It will be the week after New Year's. That gives us almost two months to get ready."

Everyone starts shouting out questions.

"What if I don't have a talent?" Kat says.

"Can we just watch?" Barry hollers.

Ms. Banta holds up two fingers again, and everyone quiets down. "You don't have to be onstage, but you are encouraged to do *something*, like make scenery or flyers and posters advertising the show. However, audience members are just as important."

My stomach unclenches. Good. No spotlight. No eyes on me.

"Do we get to miss a lot of class?" Lacey asks.

Ms. Banta laughs. "We'll use half an hour today to brainstorm and one or two other days as needed. But, save for the week before the show, all practices will be after school." Groans.

"Are there prizes?" a few people ask.

"There are no high stakes, people. No prizes. It's just for fun." Ms. Banta claps her hands. "Now then, let's take the next thirty minutes to think about your strengths. If you want to be on that stage, I'll work with you to make it happen."

Chairs scrape across the floor as everyone moves to sit next to their friends. Val drags her chair to mine.

"What can we do?" she asks, leaning over my desk, pencil *tap, tap, tapping* on my binder.

I move my binder inside my desk, wishing she'd remember that I don't like anyone touching my stuff. Even her. Her energy is making my heart *thump, thump, thump*. Val bites her lip and rolls her pencil on my desk. That's not any better than the tapping.

"How about a song?" She jiggles her legs. "Did you know my grandma played Dorothy in *The Wizard of Oz* when she was in high school? She can give us tips!"

When Val gets excited about something, it's hard to shut her down, so I don't remind her that I don't sing or do anything stagy. "Imagine how proud your grandparents will be to see you onstage. And you know Joey would love it." Joey is

Val's biggest fan. Every other word out of his mouth is about something cool Val did for him.

But Val's excitement fades, and she puts her chin in her hands. "If they even come. The school is almost three miles away. No way they're walking that far."

Now I feel bad for not thinking before I spoke. Then, I slap my forehead. I forgot the most obvious solution! "My mom and grandma can pick them all up. Problem solved!"

Val grins, but then that wavers, too. "Maybe, but the auditorium will be packed, and they're not fans of crowds." She pauses and sits straight up in her chair, face determined. "Nope," she says, shaking her head. "Not going to worry about it. It will work out."

I feel a tiny bit jealous. How is it that simple? Why can't I just decide not to worry, and then *poof*, worries be gone?!

"Anyway," she continues, "we were figuring out what to do onstage."

I laugh. "Um, no. *You* were figuring it out."

Val frowns, but then her eyes go wide as another idea takes shape. "Your dad can emcee!"

My stomach jumps, and my ankles tingle. If my dad is involved, it's harder for me to blend in.

Ms. Banta stops at our table. "I couldn't help but overhear. Having your dad emcee *was* discussed by the PTA, Maya. How would you feel about that?" She cocks her head and waits for me to answer. When grown-ups say things were "discussed," it often means "decided." I can't tell if that's the case here.

"Just think how awesome that would be!" Val says, jumping out of her seat.

I imagine Dad helping everyone with their acts and being around whenever he's needed. "Once rehearsals start, he would be here all the time," I whisper. I wouldn't have to wait until the weekend to see him.

"If that would make you uncomfortable," Ms. Banta says, "I can talk to the committee."

"N-no," I stammer. "It's fine." It's the opposite of uncomfortable. It gives me hope.

Val waits for Ms. Banta's black heels to *click clack* away before plopping down in her seat again. She pulls her chair closer. "Okay, so your dad emceeing seems to be the plan." She drums her fingers on her chair. "*But* he probably wouldn't come to that many rehearsals until it's close to crunch time. The question is," she pauses for dramatic effect and looks at me expectantly, "how do we get him involved earlier?"

I'm starting to realize what she's getting at, and I don't love it. "He'd have a reason if I were in it." What can I do that's helpful but out of the spotlight? "I could help with flyers and posters, I guess?"

Val shakes her head. "Nooo . . . Would he really need to be here after school to help you paint? And the flyer can be an email."

Being the center of attention is the last thing I want, but what if I were a sidekick? Dad could steal the spotlight, but we would still be in it together. "Maybe he and I can co-emcee?"

"Ooh, father-daughter team," Val says. "That would be really cool."

But just as I begin to picture us together onstage, reality sets in. "The PTA wouldn't allow it," I say. "Remember when Reisha's parents donated those books to the school last year, and the PTA was all snippy about a bunch of them having a special sticker with her name? They'd say I was getting special treatment and being an attention hog."

Val snickers. "Oh yeah. That's totally you."

I laugh, too. What could be further from the truth?

"What if," Val says, biting her lip, "you went up onstage by yourself?"

The tingles come in full force. "If I'm by myself, all the pressure's on me."

"That's true," Val says slowly, clearly choosing her words, "but you seem so sure you can't do it. How do you know unless you try?"

"The same way I know chocolate-covered crickets aren't for me."

Val leans in closer. "Your morning routine about you-know-who was so funny. Comedy is in your genes!"

I pull my legs to my chest and rest my chin on my knees. That wasn't the same. Val and I always joke around. Just because I like thinking of comedy bits in my head doesn't mean anyone else would find me funny. Mrs. Nelson sure wasn't cracking up at my gloves joke.

Still... for two seconds, I thought about getting up there with my dad. Maybe I *can* actually do a set myself?

I lace my fingers, moving them in and out of each other. "If I did an act, he'd be here a lot more, right?"

Val nods vigorously, and it's only green light go for her.

"And my parents would have to see each other a lot more, too."

"For sure! And he could even help with the store after rehearsals."

That would show Baba that comedy isn't a this or that. I close my eyes and imagine my family together. I'd walk off the stage, Dad would put one arm around me and the other around my mom, and he'd say, "These two ladies get me." Then, Mama would look at him and say, "You made time for Maya, and me, *and* comedy. Maybe we can meet in the middle after all." Then, Disney music would start playing, and Val would dance down the stage stairs with a string of birds behind her.

Okay, maybe not that last part. But the rest of it...

I smooth out the paper in front of me and grab a red marker before I can change my mind. Val squees when she sees the word I've written in all caps on my paper. "COMEDY."

At six o'clock, Babushka switches the sign on The Russian Gourmet to Closed, and she, Mama, and I clear out the glass cases, tidy up the shelves, and sweep the floor. The talent show permission form presses against my thigh through the pocket of my jeans. It's folded into a tiny triangle, but it feels like it's expanding by the second. By the time we sit down to dinner an hour later, all I can think about is that piece of paper, slowly slicing a million little paper cuts into my skin.

"How was school?" Babushka asks, placing a generous helping of vinaigrette salad on my plate.

This is my opening, but I shove a spoon of the tangy beet salad into my mouth to buy myself more time.

With Babushka, food always comes first, and she nods approvingly as I slowly chew. She shifts in her seat and winces as she reaches for the vinaigrette.

"Your legs?" Mama asks, concerned. "I'll get you a heating pad after dinner."

Baba shrugs. "That's what happens when you're on your feet all day. It is what it is."

No tears for her. Not for swollen legs or anything else.

"Maybe if Dad's free, he can help this weekend and give you a break," I blurt.

Babushka's fork scrapes against her plate. "If he can tear himself away from a spot. I'm sure he's dying to help."

This is where Mama normally jumps in and instructs Babushka to take it easy or throws a telling glance in my direction. Instead, she's picking at her salad, carefully spearing each little beet, potato, and pea onto her fork. Knowing how they feel about Dad's comedy, there's never going to be a good time to tell them I want to try it, too, but maybe if they knew about how involved I want Dad to be, they'd feel better about the whole thing.

I clear my throat. "So, something interesting happened today. Ms. Banta told us the school's having a sixth-grade talent show in January."

Babushka perks up. "And you want to be in it?"

"Yes—"

She claps her hands. "That's so wonderful." She elbows Mama, who returns from wherever her thoughts took her. "Isn't that wonderful, Sarah?"

Mama smiles. "Definitely. What would you like to do?"

"When I was your age," Babushka says, "I loved singing. I can work with you on that. Or maybe a Russian dance to 'Kalinka'?" She hums the quick melody, and I imagine her dancing when her body was lighter and her legs fast-moving instead of slower and swollen.

I wring my hands. "Actually, I was thinking of doing stand-up?" My voice goes up on the last word, and the decisiveness I felt when I wrote "comedy" in big red letters is nowhere to be found.

"Absolutely not," Babushka says. "You're not getting involved with that *choosh*."

"It's *not* nonsense. I can be funny!"

Mama looks from me to Babushka and slowly spreads the cheesy garlic spread on her bread.

I take her silence as an opening to keep going. "Plus, I'm pretty sure the committee is going to ask Dad to emcee."

"Sarah, are you hearing this?" Babushka spits. "Say something."

Mama takes a small bite of her bread. "It may be all right," she says softly. "It would be nice to have James around. Maya would see him more. And maybe it would get him more exposure." She places her hand over Baba's. "It could be a good thing, Mama."

Babushka pushes her chair back and begins clearing the table. She drops dirty spoons in the sink and slams the refrigerator door shut as she replaces the vinaigrette with potatoes and stewed meat. *Thump. Bang.* I jump as she plunks each dish before us.

"What do you know about performing comedy?" she asks.

"We've all seen him at the farmers' market and at that street fair last year, remember?" I say, carefully not mentioning that I've now seen him on a real club stage. "I have an idea of how it works."

Baba snorts. "The street fair where he had to shout so people could hear him, and he got upstaged by a horse with diarrhea?"

"You know he has to take all kinds of gigs to get his name out there, especially if he's trying to avoid the late-night spots."

Mama winces, and I bet she's thinking about their last fight. I've thought about it a lot, too, and how my chest felt tight when they yelled.

Then, she puts her arm around me, and a smile slowly breaks on her lips. "You know, your dad had no comedy experience when I met him. I was in the audience, and it was his first time onstage. But he made me laugh so hard. That can be you, Maya."

I lean into her elbow. "And I'll have him to help me. He didn't have that."

"He did have me," Mama says with a laugh. She nudges Baba. "Remember when he'd come over after his law school classes, and we'd sit on the porch swing and work out his jokes?"

"I remember," Baba mutters.

Mama and I talk about my act and how excited Dad will be when we tell him. "Oh my gosh," she says, snapping her fingers. "He'll have to give you his first how-to comedy book. I know he still has it."

I have never seen Mama this excited about Dad's comedy. She tells me stories about his first jokes and how he'd try to get gigs between exams. She's just remembering and not crying and . . . happy.

"Don't forget, Maya," Baba says. "He won't put your show over his gigs."

Mama sucks air through her teeth. "Just let it be."

"This will be a good thing, Baba," I say, putting my arm around her.

Babushka sighs. "You really are your mother's daughter." I know she doesn't mean it as a compliment, but I take it as one anyway. We're a team.

CHAPTER 6

On Wednesday, Barry moves his chair closer to mine, and I grip my pencils tighter and scoot my chair away.

"How are you going to do stand-up?" he says, laughing. "You're one of the most uptight people I know."

My pencils start to slip from my sweaty palms, and I shove them inside my desk. Then, I pile my books as a barrier between us and try to focus on my math work. His words prick at my eyes. I'm not "uptight." I just like things a certain way. I don't like people touching my stuff with their germy hands. No one would like that! And, yes, there's the hot-hot-hot and worries—but I can handle them. I ignore him, and Barry mumbles something about "annoying people."

"Anybody have a question?" Ms. Banta asks as she adjusts the smart board markers. Today, she's wearing a pink blouse, black pants, and pink shoes. I loosen my grip on the pencils, feeling calmer.

Four hands shoot up.

Ms. Banta helps three people, walks back to the smart board, and adjusts the markers again. Then, she helps the fourth person, two more, and it's back to the smart board.

"Ms. Banta," Derek, our resident class clown, sings as he waves his hand in the air.

She helps him, then Barry, then Reisha—three again, even though Reisha is at the other end of the room. And again, she returns to the smart board, picks up each marker, and puts it back in its holder. I stop working on my word problems and watch her more closely.

"Ms. Banta!" Derek's best friend, Matt, calls, trying to outshine Derek with his extra-loud bellow.

Ms. Banta quickly strides to his side before Val's hand shoots in the air, but there is no third, no one else begging for help. I frown. Now that I've seen it, I can't unsee it. What's with the three at a time?

I raise my hand—two seconds before Julia, who's right behind me, raises hers.

"That make sense?" Ms. Banta asks me, circling one of the numbers on my paper.

"Uh-huh," I say, but all I can think about is her next move. Will she first help Julia, who's centimeters away, or go to the board to adjust the markers?

"Great," she says, patting my arm.

Julia waves her hand like she's trying to swat a fly. Her bracelets jingle. "Ms. Banta!"

"Just one sec," she says before walking to the board.

Julia taps me on the shoulder, her dark eyebrows high on her forehead. "Is it me? Do I smell or something?"

Julia's breath *does* smell like garlic today, but I don't think that's the issue. "Maybe there's something wrong with the smart board." Or maybe it's something else. Something I'm seeing that no one else is. But why haven't I noticed before? *Was* this even a thing before?

By the end of the lesson, I've completed only half the worksheet because I've been too busy tracking Ms. Banta. Her patterns . . . Do they mean something? And if they do, what could it be?

When we arrive back at Dad's place on Saturday, he presents me with a gift. He's even wrapped it, something he *never* does. Dad's idea of wrapping is throwing the present into the first thing he finds. I've "unwrapped" pillowcases, trash bags, and empty cereal boxes. "It's what's on the inside that counts," he always says.

But here I am, holding a wrapped present, with a bow on top and everything. "Impressive."

"Your mom convinced me this one needs more fanfare." He's jumping from foot to foot like a little kid.

I tear open the wrapping paper, and there it is—the book my mom told me about.

"Yes," he says, closing his eyes, "it's the comedy bible."

The sky-blue book says *How to Get the Last Laugh* in gold letters on the cover and spine, and it's at least four hundred pages long.

"You read all of this?" I strum the pages, rubbing the worn, dog-eared paper across my fingers.

"Not all at once, but yes. It has catchphrases, timing, joke samples, how to respond to bad audiences. Everything." His eyes get teary, and he looks away. I imagine him and Mama going through this book together when he first got it, and I hug it to my chest.

He turns back to me, and his eyes aren't watery anymore, but when he speaks, his voice shakes. "I just can't believe you're doing stand-up, and I get to be there, too. When the PTA president asked me, I agreed, but now that I know you'll be in it, I actually *want* to do it."

"They're paying you the big bucks, right?"

Dad laughs. "Well, their fee will buy us a few Big Macs, at least. Maybe even an extra side of fries."

I whistle. "Fries, too? I'd say that's a fair deal. At least they didn't give you a gift certificate to our own store or something."

"Write that down," Dad says.

I whip out the spiral notebook in which I've been jotting down thoughts ever since I signed up for the show, and scribble what I said. "I don't know if that's a good joke for the show, though."

Dad shakes his head. "Doesn't matter. Just write down anything that seems funny or witty or different. Write down stuff that shows a new way of looking at something. Better to have too much and not use it than too little and be scrambling for new material."

He opens the book to the first chapter. "Let's look at joke structure. Then, we can talk about how my jokes fit in with what they say in here. After you read more at home, we'll start workshopping *your* bits. Sound good?"

I know I didn't go into this at full speed like Val would have, but having Dad talk to me like he does with his comedy buddies, like I'm not just some sixth grader doing a "cute" talent show, makes me want to dive in, too. "Sounds great!" I say as we place the book between us, the Greenspan duo at work.

CHAPTER 7

As we're walking home Monday after school, Val brainstorms talent show outfits. "I'm picturing a sparkly dress and heels, like singers wear on those reality singing competitions. That will work with whatever I sing."

"You'd pull that off for sure." She describes walking onto the stage in a sea of smoke and glitter. I don't have the heart to remind her it will more likely be a sea of painted cardboard duct-taped to black curtains.

"Ms. Banta thinks I should do a medley of Disney songs."

"That's perfect! They're your grandpa's favorite, and Disney heroines always have shimmery dresses."

While Val describes the shoes in her closet that may or may not be a perfect match, I think about Ms. Banta. I noticed the patterns again today. She was returning math homework and called out only three names at a time.

"Have you noticed Ms. Banta's three thing?" I blurt.

Val stops midsentence, not getting to finish her thoughts on whether blue pumps, pink pumps, or gold flats would best complement a sparkly dress. "What do you mean?"

"Like when she answers questions in math, she helps three people, then does something else before helping another."

Val looks at me blankly. "Does something else? Like what?"

I scrunch up my face like I'm trying to remember so it doesn't look like it's all I've been thinking about. "Well, last week she kept going back to the smart board."

Val rolls her eyes. "The smart board always has to be realigned."

"But not that many times, and she wasn't even using it."

Val shrugs. "I really wasn't paying attention. Maybe there was some tech issue."

"Maybe," I say, my voice trailing off.

Val looks at me. "Why does it matter?" She lowers her voice. "Does it have to do with the hot-hot-hot and how *you* group stuff?"

"Forget it," I mumble. "I just noticed it."

She puts her hand on my arm. "I wouldn't worry, okay? It's probably just her keeping track of who she's helped. Organizing stuff isn't bad. Gram would *kill* for my room to be more organized."

I stop walking and pretend to get something from my backpack so Val can't see my annoyed face. I know she's trying to be nice and make me feel better, but it seems like she's waving it all away and wanting everything to be normal—like when I first told her about my worries two months ago.

I was used to my mind wandering and analyzing everything. My fifth-grade teacher told my parents that I have a "scientific brain" because I always looked at experiments from all angles. But at the end of fifth grade, it started to get worse. It became more than just figuring out the best way to solve a problem. I'd get a thought in my head, and it would keep repeating. Like if I saw an ad about symptoms of some weird stomach illness, the next time I got a stomachache, my brain would jump to that disease. My palms would get sweaty, tingles would rise from my toes, and I'd just feel hot, but the hot wouldn't go away for hours. The night I overheard Baba and Mama talking about Dad's comedy, I felt the hot-hot-hot in full force, my brain unable to stop wondering why Baba said that. A month later, when Mama and Dad told me about the separation, the conversation kept replaying in my head as I lay in bed, over and over, louder and louder. I put my hands over my ears, but it didn't help. That's when I finally asked Val if she ever felt the same. We were sitting in her room, and my fingers twirled the frayed ends of her quilt.

"What do you mean?" she'd asked.

"Like do you ever just keep thinking about the same thing and can't stop?" Even saying this out loud triggered a hot feeling.

Val jiggled her foot, making the bed move and the tingles worse. "I worry about mice in the house, and when I can't fall asleep at night and hear creaking, I shut my eyes tight and hope it's not some rodent." She shuddered.

I bit the inside of my cheek. It was kind of like that. "Just the mice or you worry about other things, too?" I took a deep breath. "Because I feel like I worry about stuff all the time."

Val sat beside me on the bed. She put her hand on mine, and I noticed red indents on my fingers from where I had pulled the quilt's strings too tight. "What kind of stuff?"

I didn't really know how to put it into words. "Ummm... like getting sick? Or tests? Or... everything?"

Val chewed her lip. I took away my sweaty hand and rubbed it on my jeans. Talking about it was making things worse instead of better. "A-are you nervous now?" she stammered.

And I saw the look on Val's face. She wanted to help, but the lip chewing grew faster, and I could tell I was making *her* nervous. I took a deep breath and hoped the tingles would stop. "I'm better. Talking about it made me feel better." I gave her a hug.

She stopped chewing her lip and smiled widely. "Good." She hugged me back. "We all worry, though. You should have seen me last week when I thought I broke Joey's favorite Lego build." She raised her hands around her head and made the sound of an explosion.

After that, even though I told her more, I didn't let on how bad the hot-hot-hot had gotten and how it could start without any notice. Any time I wanted to say more, I kept picturing Val's face, her teeth grinding her lip.

So now I drag my feet as Val talks more about the show and chime in when she asks questions. Maybe Val's right, and I am reading into things because *I* like patterns and order. But Julia noticed the pattern, didn't she? No . . . She just thought Ms. Banta didn't like her breath.

When Val and I go our separate ways, I'm still thinking about Ms. Banta. Val had asked why it mattered. It shouldn't. But for some reason it does.

CHAPTER 8

"Lunch is in half an hour," Ms. Banta says two days later, "so we will be using the next thirty minutes to finalize your acts for the show. Our first after-school meeting is this Friday." She looks at her list. "I will start with Maya, Derek, and Julia." She pauses, rustles the page, and continues. "Then, I will meet with Val, Reisha, and Lacey."

Three again.

I whip my head back and try to get Val's attention, but she's too busy looking through her stack of Disney pictures. By the time she catches my eye and motions for me to join her in the reading nook, the moment has passed.

She squirms as she tries to make herself comfortable on the plastic-covered pillows in the nook. "These are really annoying," she says, making a big show of trying to plop down and get cozy, "but I know you like them."

I do love the covers. You don't have to worry about getting lice, and they're easy to clean. I inhale. "Mmm," I say. "Nothing like the smell of Lysol."

Val laughs. "You can do something with that in your act."

I write "Lysol" in my notebook, but then cross it out. I don't want to talk about the tingles or the hot-hot-hot onstage. Maybe I can say something about the Russian store and the customers. I make a note.

"Maya," Ms. Banta calls, "come share what you have."

I sit in the chair beside her and show her my notebook. "I've just been jotting down ideas."

She scans the page. "What's this Lysol thing you crossed out?"

Would she be offended if I said something about that? "I like the Lysol smell of the reading nook pillows."

Ms. Banta grins. "Maybe you can talk about some kids loving the smell of chocolate chip cookies, but for you it's Lysol?"

I shrug. "Maybe."

Ms. Banta looks at me a beat, then takes an oversize, sparkly pink pencil topper from her desk and hands it to me. "I have a blue one," she says, pointing to the one beside her book. "Whenever I'm stressed out or just can't get my thoughts together, I squeeze it to center myself." She squeezes the topper three times. "It's especially great for those gray days I need to remember my sparkle." She winks at me.

I squish the small, shiny pink blob. "Thanks," I say.

I walk back to Val clutching Pinkie (what I'll be calling the blob from now on).

"Did she help?" Val whispers.

I nod, lean back against the cushions, and add "Lysol" back to my stand-up notes.

Thursdays are our busiest days at the store because everyone wants to buy food for the weekend. Today, we added compote—a punch with fresh fruit—and plov to the mix. Plov simmers for hours, but the wait for the soft, spicy rice is worth it.

I carefully ladle the rice into a serving dish, place the new batch behind the glass, and pull the next number from the dispenser above me. "Twenty-seven!"

Everyone moves aside to make room, but no one comes. "Twenty-seven!" I call again.

People grumble and shout for me to move on. Mama calls twenty-eight just as Ms. Banta runs to the counter.

"I'm so sorry," she says breathlessly. "I couldn't find my number." She holds up a wrinkled paper with a torn twenty-seven on it.

People shake their heads in annoyance but allow Ms. Banta through.

She lowers her voice. "I have a confession. I'm a total newbie to Russian food."

"In that case," I say, grinning, "I suggest one of everything."

Ms. Banta chuckles. "You're a good salesperson. How about we start with three of your favorite things and take it from there?"

Three. My stomach flutters.

I pack quarter pounds of pelmeni, plov, and a carrot and raisin salad. "What do you think?"

Ms. Banta eyes the boxes and the food behind the case. "Looks good. What else would you suggest? My sister and her husband are visiting, and we are all big eaters." She taps her left foot three times and then does the same with her right. *Three.*

The three *has* to mean something. I play my hunch and suggest three more items. "Salad olivyeh is a big hit and pairs well with our lamb shanks and lollipop chicken."

I place all the boxes on the counter.

"You have to try our fruit compote, too," I suggest.

"That's a dessert drink?" The side of her mouth twitches. Her left foot taps. *One, two, three.*

"It is," I say, filling a container with the sweet drink.

She taps her lips with her finger. *One, two, three.* "Then throw in three pastries, too."

Three desserts.

I add three large chocolate marshmallow zephyrs and carry all the boxes to the register.

"I don't know if all of these will make it home!" Ms. Banta jokes.

"You'll just have to come back and buy more!"

She laughs. "I'll remember that." She hands Baba her credit card to pay, then digs into her wallet and leaves a few dollars in the tip jar.

"See you tomorrow, and thanks for coming!"

She waves goodbye and wraps her sleeve around her hand before opening the door.

"That was nice of her to come by," Babushka says as she moves the dollar bills from the tip jar to the register.

"What did she leave?" I ask, and Babushka raises an eyebrow. I blush, realizing how rude that sounds. "Just wondering," I mumble.

"Three dollars," she says, and now I know I've been right all along.

After the store closes, I run to my room, fling open my laptop, and Google *counting things*. The first results that come up deal with counting apps for phones. Then, there's a link for counting things in a photo. That would be useful for guessing the number of jellybeans in a jar, but not for what I need right now. Maybe I need to be more specific. I type in *counting by threes* and get a bunch of kiddie songs. Hmm . . . How about *always counting things*? **Constant Counting and OCD (Obsessive Compulsive Disorder)** is the first result that pops up. I scan the page and am launched into a rabbit hole of info.

- Counting gives people comfort and makes them feel safe.

- Some people have a "magic" number. Performing tasks around that number adds security.

Like with Ms. Banta's three.

- Organization is not a want but a *need*. Individuals with OCD may work on creating patterns.

I don't count things, but I do like organization. Val said organization is not a bad thing. I look at the page again. *Not a want, but a need.* Is it a *need*? I think about sharpening my pencils so the points are all one size and how lining them up in rainbow order calms the hot-hot-hot. I hear Barry's voice in my head. *You're the most uptight person I know.* What would happen if I just shoved the pencils into my desk like he does? I imagine a red pencil beside a green one, one perfectly sharpened, the other with a broken point. My throat tightens, and my toes tingle. The tingles lessen when I picture my dad arriving late, as always. Are these patterns? Are they *needs*? I may not have a "magic" number, but all these things make me feel "safe."

I read more, and a link sends me to **Kids: Anxiety**. I remember that word from health class and skim the page. It all comes down to how worrying can be good except when it's bad. If it gets into your head and stops you from doing things you like, that's a problem. If you think about the same stuff over and over, that's a problem.

I thought a lot about the rope burn and elastics. Problem? It was hard, but I *did* go on with my day. I go back to the OCD link. Besides counting, patterns, and wanting to keep things in a certain order, it talks about handwashing and wanting to rewash your hands, even if they're clean. Like each time I work in the Russian store and have to deal with Mrs. Nelson.

I read the pages over and feel lighter than I have in days. Each thing on its own may not mean anything, but everything together makes sense. Everything together makes *me* make sense.

I bookmark the strategies page to look at later, print out the pages, and put them in my desk drawer. I have to choose the right moment to share them with Mama and Baba. It has to be when they aren't stressed and can really listen.

For now, though, it's enough that I know there's a reason for the *whoosh* and the tingles. I don't need to prove anything to Val. Ms. Banta and I have our pencil toppers, Lysol, and patterns, and knowing someone else shares these connections makes me feel less alone.

CHAPTER 9

"Are you coming in?" I ask Dad when he drops me off in front of The Russian Gourmet after Friday's first talent show meeting. Discussing my ideas with him went so well, I want to put the next part of my plan into motion ASAP. The line stretching out the door is my chance.

"C'mon!" I say, grabbing his hand.

"Maya," he begins. He checks his watch, and my eyes dart to the impatient crowd and then back to him. Baba walks to the window and motions for me to hurry up.

"Imagine how fast we could take care of everyone if you helped," I beg. "And . . . ," I add conspiratorially, "Baba will be shocked."

"Okay, okay." He puts up his hands in surrender, and I rush out of the car.

I wash my hands, put on my apron and gloves, and run behind the counter. "Ready."

"Put me to work," Dad says, suddenly beside me. He's wearing his old apron, which seems to hang a little looser.

Mama's face lights up, and Baba's jaw drops.

"I saw a fly buzzing around earlier," Mama says to Baba. "I'd close my mouth if I were you."

Baba scowls and motions for Dad to call a number.

"Seventy," I yell at the same time Dad shouts for seventy-one. Mrs. Nelson and Mrs. Sanchez look from me to Dad.

"Karina," my dad says to Mrs. Nelson, "it's been too long. Let's catch up."

I breathe a sigh of relief as Mrs. Sanchez moves closer to my display case.

"I believe you owe him one," she says.

I laugh. "We love *all* our customers."

Mrs. Sanchez pats my cheek. "I bet you do."

As the line grows, I work faster to pack Mrs. Sanchez's containers and move them to the register.

"I heard about your big gig emceeing the kids' show," Mrs. Nelson says as Dad finishes up her order. "How cute is that?"

Dad laughs and shoves one too many pirozhki in a container. He forces it shut. "Don't ever change, Karina."

He brings her bags to the cash register and calls the next number before she can say anything else. Mrs. Nelson looks at Dad one more time, and he gives her a little wave.

"Did you get new material?" I whisper as Mrs. Nelson stalks out the door.

"One of the perks of working here," he says with a wink.

After we close the store, the four of us sit in the kitchen with cups of tea.

"How's Maya's act coming along?" Baba asks as she rubs her calves.

"I'm still reading the book and gathering ideas," I say. "But Dad and I will start workshopping soon, right?"

"Can't wait!" he says, tousling my hair. He gets a heating pad from a cabinet and gives it to Baba.

"Thank you," she says, "but I'm fine." She leaves it on the chair beside her.

Dad mumbles, "You always are."

The tingles start.

"It was nice of Dad to get you the heating pad, though, right?"

Baba shrugs. "If assuming I'm helpless is nice . . ."

Mama squeezes Dad's shoulder. "*I* thought it was nice, James." I take a sip of tea. My insides feel all warm, and the tingles begin to disappear.

Baba sighs. "I know you mean well, James, but it's nothing I can't handle." She slowly rises from the chair. "I think I'll go to bed."

When she leaves, Mama glances at her watch. "Don't you have spots?"

Dad shakes his head. "When I saw the long line at the store, I switched with a few people. I'll just go later. No big."

"Are you sure?" Mama asks. "Maya will be with you tomorrow, so you won't be able to go then either."

I'm careful not to look at Dad. Of course he'll be at spots tomorrow.

"Don't worry about it, Sarah. It's all good." His dimple pops in his cheek, and Mama relaxes.

I bang the table with my hands. "It's settled then."

Mama and Dad exchange amused looks.

I make my face serious. It's time to take Operation Reunite Mama and Dad up a level. "We have something important to discuss." I pause. "Catchphrases."

Mama taps her fingers on the table. "You don't *need* one, right, James?"

Dad thinks about it. "It's not something comics need, but when you're starting out, it can definitely be an easy way to transition between jokes."

I nod. "That's what the comedy bible says. I think it would help me ground the jokes and create their . . ." I try to think of what the book called it. I snap my fingers. "Their framework."

Mama grins. "Dad had that down. His name is James, and he don't play games."

They both start laughing, and Dad hides his face behind his hands. "Nooo," he groans.

"What does that even mean?" I look from one to the other. Mama wipes tears from her eyes, she's laughing so hard. "How is that a catchphrase?"

"It's not," Dad says, peeking out from behind his fingers. "But it was my first attempt to transition from one joke to another."

"He threw in a karate kick for good measure, too," Mama says.

"Stop!" I squeal. "You did not!"

Mama opens her mouth to speak, then starts giggling again. I laugh. "I feel better now. Talk about lowering the bar."

"All right, all right," Dad says, faking a stern face. "This is important."

Mama pushes her cheeks together, trying to erase her smile. "I'm ready. Go."

"So," I say, "I was looking through the comedy book, and it gave sample catchphrases for starting out. What about 'Ain't that the truth'?"

Dad wrinkles his nose. "That won't really work with your ideas."

I think about my notes. *There's this boy in my class . . . Ain't that the truth.* "Yeah, you're right."

"I kind of like the *ain't*, though," Mama says, finally composed.

Dad rubs his chin. "That's so out of character for you, it makes it funny."

"True. What else?" I tap my chin and glance at Mama and Dad, who are just happy and smiling. Just like I imagined this night would go.

"'Ain't it grand'?" I offer, remembering a phrase I heard in one of Val's Disney movies.

Dad gives me a thumbs-down. "When did you become royalty?"

Mama taps a finger to her lips. "Your jokes are about things you notice every day, right?"

I nod.

"So, you need a lead-in that goes with that. Like 'Ain't it . . .'" She taps her lips again.

"Wait!" I say. I run to get the book and open it to the table of contents. "Here it is! They have a section here on what they call 'Observational Humor,' and they start with 'Isn't it funny . . .' So I could do 'Ain't it funny'!"

"Yes!" Dad says. "That works."

"Teamwork," Mama says.

"His name is James, and he don't play games," I chime in.

Mama bursts out laughing, and Dad slinks low in his seat. And ain't it funny how my tingles are gone, and it's all working out?

CHAPTER 10

At the talent show practice the following week, Dad and I sit side by side in the back of the auditorium, my notebook and comedy bible between us. Now that I have a catchphrase and a week of observations in hand, I'm ready to start workshopping my jokes.

Dad reads through my notes, nodding eagerly and circling stuff on the page. "Let's start here," he says once he's had a few minutes. He points to the joke I told Val about Barry. "This image of squirreling away pencils is great, but it needs more punch."

"Punch? What do you mean?" My heart races. I know jokes take time to create. I've heard Dad tell the same joke to different audiences, changing small things to make it as funny as possible. But still, I'm nervous I won't get it right. That I don't have *it*. And if I don't have *it*, then I'll bomb onstage and Mama will continue to think that comedy isn't a real dream. "Val thought it was funny," I mumble.

Dad pulls me to him. "It *is* funny. We just have to refine it and pin down your voice."

I don't know what he means exactly, but my heartbeat slows. I move closer to him. "How would *you* 'refine' it?"

"Let's talk it through." He flips the pages of the comedy bible to a chapter I bookmarked called "Crafting a Joke." He taps the page. "Have you studied it?"

"Not only that," I say, closing my eyes, "but I've become the book."

"All right then!" he says. "What's our first step?"

I open my eyes and flip through my notebook. "Focusing on a specific moment." I think about Barry and my pencils but quickly stop.

I lower my voice. "Barry bugs me, but I don't want to hurt his feelings."

Dad rubs his chin. "For sure. But, if I'm right about the Barrys of the world, he'll love it. He'll be a star." Dad mimes Barry's name over an imaginary marquee. "Tell you what, though. Let's figure out the joke first, and then once you have the bones, you can tweak it if you think it's too much."

I give him a thumbs-up. "Got it."

He's giving me his full attention. I've seen that look when he's bounced material back and forth with Mama and his comic friends. He's looking at me like someone in the biz, not just his daughter.

I scan the room for Barry and find him a mile away by the stage curtain. I look at the notes I jotted. "I was thinking of this one time when he reached over my stuff and snagged my bundle of pencils."

Dad looks confused. "Like, just grabbed them all?"

I nod. "Yup. He gave all but one back, but it was weird. It was almost like he just took them and then was all, 'Wait, what do I need all these for?'" It's kind of funny to think about it now.

Dad laughs. "Huh, okay. There has to be a way to connect that to something bigger."

I think about it. "What about the idea of FOMO? Like he's scared of missing out and takes more than he needs? Like at a Black Friday sale. People grab extra things they don't need because of the deals. All wild-eyed."

He nods eagerly, writes "wild eyes, sale" in my notebook. "Great! Someone grabbing pencils with that level of frenzy is where the funny is. And you had that great squirrel comparison, too, because everyone can picture squirrels hoarding their acorns. Can all of it be combined somehow?"

I wring my hands. "I get what you're saying, but I don't know how that would work."

His eyes glimmer. "How about you go with the sale metaphor and the frenzied look? Besides Black Friday, when else do people get all chaotic at stores?"

I got it! "When there's a snowstorm coming! Remember last year when all the big supermarkets closed and our store was still open? Mrs. Nelson was shouting about 'more milk!' and we ran out of bread?"

"That's perfect," Dad says. "Now you have to find a way to use that comparison to make Barry's actions feel even bigger and set the scene."

I bite the inside of my cheek, trying to figure it out. "I want to use the catchphrase, but it doesn't quite work with what I want to say."

"I've been thinking about that. Catchphrases should come naturally. If they work, and help you transition, great. But if not, you shouldn't force it."

That takes some of the pressure off. I grab an imaginary mic. "Everyone has that thing they can't get enough of. Video games, chocolate, ice cream. But for this one kid in my class, it's pencils! He stashes them like he's preparing for the next blizzard." I feel the electricity popping around me.

Dad writes as I speak. "That's a great beginning. Now, can we double down on the blizzard scenario? Maybe with your bread and milk observation?"

"Don't worry about the bread and milk, ShopRite. You better lock down the school supply aisle."

"Love it!" Dad writes more, then pauses. "I don't want you to lose the squirrel part, though. That was really funny. What about after *You better lock down the school supply aisle*, you pause, look concerned, and say something that connects to squirrels. Um, maybe, 'But where is he putting all those pencils?'"

I leap up. *"But where is he stashing them? Has anyone checked the tree by his house? I bet there are some angry squirrels losing prime acorn space!"*

Dad punches his fist in the air. "Yes! Yes!"

Kids working on the stage stop what they're doing and look in our direction, but this time I don't care. I'm too happy.

"Wow," I say, sitting back down. "Is this how it feels each time you figure out a joke?"

He gives me a bear hug. "Yup. Isn't it awesome?"

I nod but get a little deflated when I remember what he said about tweaking the joke. "It's not over, though, right? You have to keep fine-tuning to make it even better."

Dad rubs his chin. "Yes, but I love doing that, because then I get this same feeling over and over again."

I grin. "It's a little like how when you, Mama, and I came up with the catchphrase. That was a good feeling, too."

Dad smiles. "Your mom was my good-luck charm. She used to go to each show . . ." His voice fades. The part that gets left out is *until she didn't*. Except with my plan, maybe she can become his good-luck charm again.

"Well, wouldn't it be cool if we all workshopped the jokes together? You can come to the next after-school practice, stay for dinner . . ."

Dad looks nervous. "I don't know, Maya. I'm happy to come to practices, of course, but you, me, Mama, and Baba . . ."

"Mama would be into it, I know it." I think she would. I *hope* she would.

He squirms.

I grab *How to Get the Last Laugh*. "I solemnly swear on this book of the best jokes ever that I'm telling the truth."

Dad leans back in the chair. "Clearly you're serious."

"I am." I clasp the book. "And if you helped with the store, you'd be the most favorite person in the house."

"Aha!" he says, raising his finger in the air. "There it is. You just want less face time with the customers."

I giggle. "You got me."

He grins and shakes his head. "Okay, okay. Store and jokes. We'll figure it out."

"Mr. Greenspan," Lacey says, running up to us, "can you puh-leeease help me with my poem? I need that oomph to make it sing onstage."

Before Dad can respond, Val runs past Lacey and tugs on Dad's sleeve. "My songs are falling flat. They need pizzazz or something."

"Your public needs you," I say, giving him a hug.

He gives me a small salute, then walks away with Val and Lacey to help them with their dreams. Working in the store will help Mama with hers. Then, when my family is back together for good, my dream will come true, too.

CHAPTER 11

"Mmm . . . ," I say, walking in the front door a few days later. The smell of sufganiyot, special Chanukah jelly-filled doughnuts, fills the house.

Babushka and Mama closed the store early today so they could get ready for the first night of Chanukah.

"Did you leave me any dough?" I wash my hands and take a bite out of a large powdered doughnut. The thick jelly oozes across my lips.

"Of course," Mama says. "Wouldn't be Chanukah without your famous cinnamon jelly doughnuts."

I stand between Mama and Babushka and grab a rolling pin. I push the wooden rod across the top of the dough, then toward me, then to the left and the right. It always amazes me how you can begin with a small ball and have a mass three times that size when it's rolled out. I cut the rolled pieces into strips. Once the pieces look like thick strings, I add sugar, cinnamon, and a layer of jelly, and then shape them into pinwheels.

"My mother made these every Chanukah," Babushka says. "She never missed a year. Even when she had to hide being Jewish, she'd just pull down the shades and keep going. There was another year when cinnamon was nonexistent.

Your great-grandma woke up before dawn and walked five miles each way to buy it at the black market."

"You're the same way, Mama," my mother says. "You don't let anything stop you. Remember when I was ten and you stood in line for five hours to get me that Cabbage Patch doll?"

Babushka laughs. "I don't think I'd put that in the same category as surviving Stalin."

I roll out more dough and put raspberry jelly inside it. Tomorrow, we'll sell these at our store, too. Dad's favorites are with grape jelly, so I make extras of those.

"And *your* mama," Babushka says to me, kneading out the dough, creating a perfect circle with her fingers, "once drove three hours to find you apricots because they were out of season, but she heard some store down the shore had them."

Mama taps my nose with her floured hand. "One day, *dochenka*, you'll be doing the same for your daughter."

"Nothing can stop us. You remember that," Babushka says, winking. "We're tough."

I must have been six or seven, but I remember that day differently. "Didn't Dad go with you to get the apricots?"

Before Mama can answer, Babushka jumps in. "Oh, he went, all right, but he left your mama to do the bargaining while he chased down club managers for an evening spot."

Mama places a hand on Baba's arm. "It was fine. As you say, we women are strong. Anyway, I *wanted* him to go."

My stomach clenches, and a faint *whoosh* starts in my head, ready to grow louder. I can't squeeze Pinkie, so I focus on rolling the dough, sprinkling the cinnamon, and adding the jelly, like a human conveyor belt. I've been noticing something. The first time I felt the *whoosh* and tingles getting worse was after Mama and Dad's separation talk. Whenever Mama and Dad argue, the feelings blow up, too. But . . . when Dad, Mama, and I were talking about catchphrases, they lay low. I didn't notice them in the store the last time Dad was there either. I stop rolling. Is it all connected? Could getting my parents back together also stop the hot-hot-hot? That idea makes my plan more important than ever.

"When's Dad getting here?" I blurt.

Mama stops rolling. "He's not."

The tone of her voice freezes me. "Not even for a little while?" I want to smush the grape jelly doughnuts I made for him. Didn't he say he would work something out? If he can't do that for Chanukah, what hope is there he'll do it for the store? "He couldn't switch for an early or late-night spot?"

Babushka rolls harder. "He wouldn't have switched even if we'd asked him."

I look at the two of them and silently apologize to the grape jelly doughnuts. "You didn't invite him?"

Mama bites her lip and goes back to rolling. "He wasn't here for Thanksgiving either."

She's right, but Thanksgiving has never been a huge event for us. We always keep the store open late and then eat leftovers we prepared the night before. I just figured he booked spots that day because it didn't matter.

"But it's Chanukah!" I say. How do they not understand it's a big deal? "We all had fun when he was here last week. He even helped with the store. Now he's going to be all alone."

Baba pushes hard with her rolling pin, and the dough tears. "He'll be fine, Maya."

Mama bites her lip and keeps rolling the dough.

I bang my hands on the pin and send bits of flour dust into the air.

"Honestly, Maya," Baba says, annoyance creeping into her voice. "Stop with the drama." I raise my hands to bang the pin again, but Baba gives me a hard stare.

"I'm going to the bathroom."

In the bathroom, I wash my hands and whip out my phone to call Dad. I leave the water running to muffle my voice.

"Happy Chanukah, kiddo," Dad says before I can speak. "Making jelly doughnuts?"

I clutch the phone. Hearing his voice makes me even sadder that he's not here. "When are you coming?"

He pauses, then stammers, "Well, uh, I don't think I am. It's a special time for you and your mom—"

"It should be a special time for *all* of us," I say, cutting him off. "Mama, Baba, and I were just talking about you coming." That's not a lie at all. That is technically what happened before I left to use the bathroom.

"Really?" Dad says, and the hope in his voice makes me feel a little guilty. Still, I keep going because I *know* Mama looked upset. I *know* she misses him and would be psyched if he came.

"Yep! I'm making the special sufganiyot for you." When he's quiet, I add, "So you'll come?"

"I already have spots tonight, but I'll be there tomorrow. I just have to check with your mom."

"No, you don't!" I sputter.

Dad laughs. "I do, but it sounds like she'll be okay with it, right?"

"Definitely." I make my voice grape jelly sweet. "See you tomorrow!"

My mood picks up as I wash my hands and skip back to the kitchen. "I'm sorry for being grumpy, Baba," I say, gently lifting the rolling pin and pushing it over the dough.

Just then, Mama's phone buzzes. She peeks at it, wipes her hands on her apron, and walks out of the kitchen. When she returns a few minutes later, she raises her eyebrows at me. I can tell she's hiding a smile.

"That was James," she says. "Turns out Maya was right about him not wanting to be alone on Chanukah. I told him he's always welcome."

If I knew how to do a cartwheel, I'd do one right now. Mama said yes! And the sad look she had before I went to the bathroom is gone, too! All my parents need is to spend more time together and remember all the good times. I whistle and roll the dough. My stomach is clench-free, my head is *whoosh*-free, and my feet are tingle-free. I think my hunch was right. This show can fix *all* our problems.

Baba throws up her hands. "Let's hope he doesn't cancel."

"He won't," I sing. "Didn't he keep his promise with the first talent show meeting?"

Baba breathes deeply through her nose, then puts her arm around me. "You're right. He did."

I imagine the menorah glowing in the window, the gleam from its electric lights brightening our faces, as we all sit together with grape jelly coating our lips.

CHAPTER 12

"Chanukah Harry has arrived!" Dad booms as soon as we open the door the next night.

Even Baba bursts out laughing at his outfit. He's wearing a blue sweater with a huge latke on it and blue jeans with painted multicolored dreidels. He has garbage bags in both hands.

"I see you brought your laundry, James," Babushka says, but I can tell she's teasing.

"Just want to feel at home," Dad says. I hope a part of him really means it.

"We waited for you to make the latkes." I give him a hug.

He puts the bags on the floor and rolls up his sleeves. "Show me the way."

The three of us go into the kitchen as if this year is the same as all the others. Babushka, Mama, Dad, and I grab peelers and graters. We never use a food processor, even though it's quicker. Dad gripes about that every year, but today he looks happy.

"Any new bits?" Dad asks me as I scrape my peeled potato over the grater. Pieces of pulp fall into a bowl.

"I'm workshopping the one about The Russian Gourmet." I peel and grate the onion and use paper towels to drain the extra liquid from the mixture.

"You can't be making fun of our customers, Maya," Baba says.

"Maya's got it covered," Dad says. "Right?" He bumps my hip with his.

I bump it back. "Yup. No one will be upset, Baba. Trust me." I give her a kiss on the cheek and add egg to the potato and onion mush.

Babushka shakes her head and goes back to grating.

"How about you, James?" Baba asks. "Have you been discovered yet?"

I tense, and Dad does, too. Babushka isn't teasing this time. Her words have bite.

I pour oil into a pan and bring my bowl of potato mush to the stove. Pinkie presses against my hip bone, and I turn my back on my family and practice breathing like I did in the Brody's bathroom. *Breathe in for four, hold for four, breathe out for four. Four, four, four.* The oil sizzles, and I open my eyes as it *pop, pop, pops* and jumps from the pan into the air.

"Not yet, Clara," Dad says, scraping his onion on the grater. "But fingers crossed, right?"

Mama clears her throat. "Maya mentioned Artie Munch saw you?"

I spin around and connect my gaze with Dad's. I give my head a slight shake, hoping he'll understand I didn't tell Mama I was at the club with him, only about Artie.

Pop, pop, pop.

Dad frowns. I know he doesn't want to keep secrets from Mama. "A few times now. I guess he hasn't made up his mind yet."

I scoop the mixture with my hands and drop the batter into the pan.

"Well, I'm rooting for you," Mama says. Baba snorts in response.

I open my mouth to say Baba should have heard the applause but force the words back.

No one says anything anymore. We just keep grating in silence except for the growing *whoosh* in my head and the constant *pop, pop, pop* of the oil trying to break free.

After dinner and lighting the Chanukah menorah, Babushka sits down on the couch and rubs her legs.

"Long day?" Dad asks.

"It always is," she says, pulling over a stool to prop up her feet.

"There's another talent show meeting next week, so I'll move things around to help with the store again."

Babushka takes a deep breath and slowly lets it out. "Sure, James. If you can fit it in."

Why does she have to doubt him? "He said he'd do it," I say through clenched teeth as a *whoosh* swirls in my head.

Dad puts his hand on my shoulder and gives it a squeeze. "Why don't we see what Chanukah Harry brought?"

He hands me three gifts, and I tear the wrapping paper off each one. There's a book about comic greats, an electronic notetaker for school since my phone has to be shut off, and an assortment of sparkly lip balms. "I love all of this!" I say, giving him a big hug. "And you wrapped them, too!"

Dad grins. "That's from your mom and Baba also."

"You can keep recipes on that device, too," Babushka says, pointing to the notetaker. "That's what *I* wanted it for . . ."

I give her a kiss. "I'll use it for recipes, too."

Mama looks at the clock. "We should probably start cleaning up."

"I have more gifts," Dad says.

Her face reddens. "But we said only for Maya. I didn't—"

"I wanted to," he insists. He gives wrapped boxes to Baba and Mama.

Mama laughs when she opens hers. It's an apron with a muscular woman on it. "Cooking Is Strength," it says.

"There's another box," Dad says.

"Oh, now I feel horrible," Mama says, opening the box. There's a little charm of a chef's hat.

Babushka's face softens when she opens her gift.

"Compression socks," Dad says. "They should help your legs."

"That was very nice of you, James." She gets off the couch and starts heading to the kitchen.

"I don't have a spot tonight," he says. "Sarah and I will clean up. You go rest."

Baba catches Mama's eye and tilts her head ever so slightly in Dad's direction. "You can manage without me, Sarah?"

Mama smiles and nods, and Baba, after looking back at Mama one last time, walks slowly up the stairs.

"Maya, you better get ready for bed, too," Mama says.

I hug them both good night and rush halfway up the stairs before tiptoeing back down a few steps. Dad wipes down the table while Mama piles the dishes in the sink. They take turns washing the pans as the glow from the menorah casts a shadow on the wall.

This is how it happens. They're hanging out just like they used to before they started fighting about Dad's spots. And Dad didn't even book a spot for tonight. I think about Mama's support of me and how much she laughed when we brainstormed catchphrases. She's starting to see why Dad loves comedy so much, I can feel it.

I creep to my room, change into my pajamas, and lie down. I close my eyes and imagine myself onstage, Mama and Baba in the front row, Dad's eyes meeting Mama's from across the school auditorium. The *whoosh* is a faint ghost now. I close my eyes and dream of our family together, my head free of noise.

CHAPTER 13

On Monday, I'm still bundled in my Chanukah glow, but the layers slowly unravel when I walk into McKinley. There's something off in the air, little things that no one else seems to notice. Like the way Ms. Banta's voice is higher pitched than usual when she tells us to put our backpacks in our lockers. Or the fact that her clothes don't match.

But the girls are all oohing and aahing about her pink scarf and yellow shoes.

"It's a little too springy for the cold weather, but you gotta admire the fashion risk!" Val says.

"Ms. Banta doesn't take risks," I mutter. She has patterns.

Everything feels loud. The chatter, the *whoosh*, the bell. I cover my ears.

"What's wrong?" Val mouths, or maybe says. It's hard to tell. "Are you all right?"

I slowly put my hands down. "Isn't the bell loud today?"

She shrugs. "It's loud *every* day." But she studies me, biting her lip. "Is it the hot thing? I thought you had a great weekend."

"I did," I say. "It's not that." I don't know how to explain what's going on because I don't get it myself. Why does it matter if Ms. Banta looks different? My weekend was perfect.

Why isn't that feeling carrying over? My fingers tingle, and I wrap an arm tightly around my books while my other hand searches my binder for Pinkie.

"I can take you to Ms. Graham," Val says, gnawing faster on her lip.

I give her what I hope is a convincing smile. "You're the best, but I'll be okay. I think it's the weather. It was so cold outside, but it's so warm in here." Wow. I'm a regular Mrs. Nelson.

Val perks up. Her teeth release her lip. "That must be it. Sometimes this school is too hot. That happens to me, too." *See? We're the same. We all worry.* She gives me a quick hug before jogging to her desk.

"Class," Ms. Banta says, "please take out your math journals."

I glance at the board, relieved to see the regular daily schedule.

The *whoosh* quiets, and I shove my pencils into my desk, careful not to leave any within Barry's reach. I don't want anything to restart the tingles.

"Please continue with PEMDAS," Ms. Banta says, taking a green smart board marker from its stand. She writes a few examples on the board.

I follow the rules. Parentheses, Exponents, Multiplication or Division (the trick is to remember to do whichever comes first), Addition or Subtraction (whichever is first). It's easy to do the problems and not get fooled if you just stick to the steps. Parentheses are always done first, no matter where they appear. Patterns.

"You're so slow," Barry mutters. "I'm on page two already."

"It's not a race." I clutch my pencils tightly and press harder on my paper. Following PEMDAS lessens the hot-hot-hot.

"Raise your hand if you're still working on page one," Ms. Banta says.

I don't look up to see how many hands are raised, and I don't raise mine either.

Barry pokes me in the ribs, and my pencil skids across the paper onto the desk. "Tell her you're still on page one," he hisses.

"Leave me alone," I whisper back, and slowly erase the stray pencil marks off my desk.

"Maya is still on page one!" Barry shouts.

I grit my teeth and try to find a stand-up way to spin this. *And this kid next to me is all in my business like he's in the FBI or something. What does he care? [Remember to pause.] If the FBI is really that worried about a sixth-grade worksheet, I think we all have bigger problems.*

"Don't worry," Ms. Banta says, suddenly beside me. "Take your time."

I nod and squeeze Pinkie.

"I'm almost on page three, Ms. Banta!" Barry screeches.

"That's good, Barry," Ms. Banta says. Her voice sounds far away. "Be sure to check your work."

Pencils scribble around me. Barry bangs into my desk, grinning as he ruins my carefully crafted numbers.

Hands shoot up, and Ms. Banta hesitates before approaching anyone, like she's trying to decide what to do. I give up on my math and watch her, hoping my brain was just playing tricks before and nothing's wrong. But I quickly see it wasn't my imagination running wild. Something's up. Her patterns are all off. Sometimes, she answers two students before going back to the smart board. Other times, she goes back after three. And still others, she doesn't go back at all, just goes from one kid to another.

Her left hand stays at her side as she fidgets with her blue pencil topper. I see her being pulled to the smart board, an imaginary string tugging at her waist, but she resists it. Why is she resisting?

When math ends, I've only completed one and a half pages. Ms. Banta's eyes dart to the clock, and she panics.

"Oh my," she says, trying to keep her voice light, "we went ten minutes over."

"I hope this doesn't mean less time for creative writing," Val pouts. "I was going to work on my act. That's creative, right?"

"Sure," I squeak. Ms. Banta *never* makes mistakes like this.

As Ms. Banta tries to transition to creative writing, I take out my notepad and stylus. I think about another tip from the stand-up book.

<u>THE RULE OF 3.</u>

As part of your joke, you give the audience a list of three things. For the first two items, give them what they're anticipating. Then, for the third thing, knock their socks off with something unexpected. The key to humor is in the unpredictable—the element of surprise.

It wasn't my favorite bit of advice, but now I write it down, hoping it can help me make sense of what's happening. The words seem to grow on my screen until no white space remains. **Break patterns for best results.**

CHAPTER 14

"It's a pattern with him," Babushka tells Mama two days later as she chops beets for the borscht.

Stomach rumbling, I came down for a snack and study break, but as soon as I realized they were talking about Dad, I hid behind the kitchen doorway.

"Mama, please. He hasn't missed a weekend with Maya since he moved out. Plus, he said he's trying to work things out with this gig."

Babushka's knife sashays across the wooden cutting board. "He never moved spots when he lived here. Why would he cancel one now when he's following his 'dream'?"

The way she says *dream* makes my skin prickle. She supports Mama's dream. Why does Dad's dream bother her? Would she approve of *my* dream for our family?

I go back to my room and call Dad. "I hear you're ditching me this weekend," I say as soon as he picks up. It's supposed to sound jokey, but the bitterness in my voice surprises me.

"Wow," he says. "Harsh words."

A lump forms in my throat. My eyes burn. "Aren't you?" I whisper.

Dad's breath is heavy over the phone. "It's not *you*. You know how much I love spending time with you."

"I know." We both stay silent. "Is it another Artie opportunity? Hasn't he seen you a bunch of times already?"

Dad groans. "My thoughts exactly, but that's how some managers work."

I don't say anything. I think about the annoyance in Baba's voice. It's only one weekend, though, and he'll still be at Friday's talent show practice and help with the store afterward. And then I realize she wouldn't be as annoyed if that were true. "You're booked the whole weekend, aren't you? This means no Friday practice either?"

It's Dad's turn to be silent. "I'm really sorry, but it's just this one time. This is a slow process, sweetheart. But if it pans out, the sky's the limit."

For one painful second, I feel the same disappointment and hurt that Mama and Baba always seem to have with Dad. Doesn't he understand that if he misses this practice, he's just proving them right? But then I take a deep breath. *Think of the big picture, Maya.* It's *one* missed practice. *One* missed weekend. Each one brings him a step closer to Artie and his dream.

"Why stop at the sky?" I say, trying to push the anger sparks to the pit of my stomach.

I hear Dad's smile through the phone when he says, "That's right. Infinity and beyond, and then fancy meals for all."

"But I like the hole-in-the-wall pizza places we visit."

Dad laughs. "I'll be doing so well, we'll be eating pizza with truffles that costs ten bucks a slice."

I wonder if he's including Mama in that "we." "I'll hold you to that."

"I love you, kid. I'll make next weekend extra special."

When we hang up, I open the comedy book and look at another tip.

THE CALLBACK

1. A callback is when a comic brings up an idea they mentioned earlier in the set.
2. Some may disagree, but we think bringing it up three times is magic. First, the audience is introduced to the idea, then you refer to it in the middle of your set, and then BAM. You wow them by talking about it again at the end.
3. But don't stress if you can't manage the three. At least two will do.

Now, wait here, you're probably yelling. **You told me I should BREAK patterns!** What can we say? Who told you to listen to a bunch of comedians?

Why has everything been so off these last few days? Ms. Banta suddenly decided to throw all her patterns out the window. Now, Dad is missing not only talent show practice but a whole weekend with me. I flop down on my bed. Can I get a callback to when everything made sense?

CHAPTER 15

On Friday, Ms. Banta instructs us to go to our read-ing spots. I grab Pinkie and shuffle to the back of the room. The plastic seat covers don't have their comforting Lysol smell.

"Ms. Banta," I say, "can I please read at my desk?"

She looks through me. "Sure, Maya."

But when I get to my desk, I don't read. I arrange my pencils by color, then by size. I peek at Ms. Banta, but her eyes are glued to her pencil topper as her fingers squeeze and release it.

Barry gets up from his spot on the cushions and strolls to the garbage. He walks too close to my desk, and I scramble to shove my pencils into my pencil case.

He snorts and keeps on walking. His hand brushes the side of my desk. *In, two, three, four. Out, two, three, four.*

Then, he's back on the rug, his body stretched out on the cushions, book in hand, like his whole goal of throwing out his trash had nothing to do with me.

I place my pencil case inside my desk and focus on my breathing. My head is filled with noise and fog. I want to punch some dough, curl up in my bed, and stare at the ceiling while the hours fast-forward to tomorrow. Maybe he did just want to throw something out. Maybe messing with me was just a bonus.

I run my fingers along the grooves on the side of my desk. They press against something soft, wet, and rubbery. I look down, and the *whoosh* surrounds me. The tingles return, prickling my toes, legs, and fingers all at once.

Gum. Bright orange, newly chewed, is stuck to my fingertips. I hold my hand out in front of me, like it's a bomb about to go off. I have seconds to get that slimy, sticky goo off my fingers before it detonates. I run to the trash can and shake my hand over it, but it won't come off. It's bad enough that one hand is already contaminated; I don't want to use my other hand and infect it, too.

"Maya?" Ms. Banta asks, placing a hand on my shoulder. "Are you all right?"

Tears push at my eyelids, and I shake my head no. *Barry*, I mouth showing her my hand, and she sprints to her desk for tissues.

Her lips pucker as she uses a Kleenex to remove the gum. It falls into the bin, and orange peeks out from the white tissue.

"Thank you," I whisper. Ms. Banta's face is pale as she wipes her hands on her red sweater.

"Sanitizer," she breathes, and she crosses the room in two strides, her brown shoes thumping on the tiles. She pushes the pump *one, two, three* times and rubs the clear liquid into her palms and fingernails. She's about to pump some onto my hands, too, but I show her my cracked skin.

"Scrub them well," she says as she writes out a bathroom pass.

A few students look up but then go back to reading. It's like Ms. Banta and I are in our own little play.

As I walk to the door, she calls Barry's name, her voice sharp. I turn around and watch her squirt another three pumps of sanitizer into her hands as she paces back and forth.

CHAPTER 16

I don't know how many times I washed my hands yesterday to remove Barry's germs, but they're so dry, I flinch when they brush against anything.

"Are you feeling okay?" Mama asks when I walk into The Russian Gourmet kitchen. She and Baba both place hands on my forehead to check for fever.

"You're not warm," Baba says.

"Are you upset you're not seeing your dad tonight?" Mama asks, stroking my hair. "That must be hard."

What's hard is that there's now a crack in my plan, and I'll have to make up the lost time. Just thinking about this makes my hands burn. They beg to be washed again even though I'm wearing gloves. I put them behind my back, hoping the out of sight, out of mind saying is true, but not giving in to the urge makes it worse. My heart beats quickly, and my chest tightens. Maybe if I share the Google pages, Mama and Baba can help me think of ways to deal with this, too. "Be right back."

I run to my room and grab the pages from my desk. "Can you guys sit?"

Baba and Mama wipe their hands on their aprons and sit beside me.

"I wanted to show you both something." I hand the printout to Mama.

Baba's and Mama's eyes flit between the pages and each other, and I realize I didn't think this through. What if they can't help? What if they think feeling this way is my fault?

Mama finally places the pages back on the table, but it's Baba who speaks first. "Is this about that show?" She gets up, washes her hands, and goes back to kneading cookie dough. "I knew it was a bad idea. Just because it's in your father's head—"

"The show?" How did she make that leap?

Mama frowns at Babushka. "It can be about the show. It's normal to be nervous—"

"It's not about the show." My stomach clenches, and the tingles start.

Babushka punches the dough harder. "Is this for a school project?"

I made a big mistake. They can't help it if this is totally out of the blue for them. They don't know anything about the hot-hot-hot or the tingles or my germ issues. For me, these pages helped name my feelings. For them, it's a school report they didn't ask to read. I see they only skimmed the first two pages, so I give Mama the heading I should have started with in the first place. **Kids: Anxiety**.

"What does it say?" Baba asks as she tears a piece of dough, rolling it into a ball and pressing her thumb in the center.

Mama puts up one finger and keeps reading, and Baba makes huffing noises as she rips more dough.

Finally, Mama says, "Maya, you think this is you?"

I nod. "There are matches."

Babushka wipes her hands on her apron and comes back to the table. She snatches the papers and shakes her head as she reads. "This isn't you." Her finger scans the page. "See? You don't lie awake all night just thinking, do you?"

"No," I say. "But—"

"And here," Mama says, pointing to another section, as if Baba's pointing has given her permission to take a stand, too. "It talks about not wanting to go to school. That's not you."

"No," I agree, "but did you read this part?" I tap the section about wanting things organized a certain way. "I always feel better when my pencils are lined up."

Babushka laughs. "You should have seen this one." She swings her head in Mama's direction. "When she was your age, every outfit had to be matchy-matchy."

Mama giggles, remembering. "And ask your father about his lucky tie."

The tingles get worse. What if they're right? I was clinging to these pages like they had the answer to everything. What if what's going on with me has no name or solution?

"Maya," Babushka says, putting her floured hands on my shoulders, "I'm afraid our family is just *razborchivie*."

"It's not just being *picky*," I insist. A low rushing sound forms in my ears. Like a plane taking off far away. *Whoosh*.

"You're fine," Mama says, hugging me. "That's just our genes."

Why does only Ms. Banta realize this might be something else?

Mama gently takes my hand. "Come help us with the dough. That always calms me when I worry."

Babushka agrees. "There's nothing like a good kneading to soothe the nerves. And that's all it is, *Zaichik*. Remember, the women in our family are strong. Nothing gets the best of us."

"Sometimes we worry too much, but—" Mama says.

"That's just because we care," Babushka finishes, kissing the top of my hair.

I'm about to protest and ask about my germ stuff, but Babushka will say that's just because I care about our customers.

I put on new gloves and trudge to the kitchen island. Babushka drops a clump of dough beside me, and I bury my gloved fists deep in the soft mass. I watch as Babushka and Mama rip chunks from the body, make them into tiny balls, then press them gently with their thumbs, leaving small prints in each cookie. I do the same, then place each piece on a baking sheet.

Knead, roll, thumbprint. I repeat the steps until the tingles lessen and the *whoosh* is gone. When all the cookies have been placed in the oven, I take the Google pages back to my room and pull up the bookmarked strategies page. I read the page over and over. It doesn't matter if this totally describes me or not. I need something to follow, like a paint-by-numbers thought guide just for me. Especially if my plan is teetering on a tightrope.

I look at a tip that worked before. "Create a calming mental image," it reads. I lie on my bed and close my eyes, imagining my fists punching the dough, my fingers pulling the strands and rolling them into tiny balls.

I think about what Babushka said about the women in our family being strong. Strong women don't give in to worry.

I grab Pinkie out of my backpack and give it a squeeze. Ms. Banta would tell me to remember my sparkle. Maybe she'd say my kind of worry—*our* kind of worry—is special.

"Maya!" Mama calls. "Come eat something before Baba and I go back to the store."

I drag myself downstairs, imagining a sea of glitter creating a trail behind me.

CHAPTER 17

"You're late," Babushka says when I run into The Russian Gourmet Sunday morning. "Hairnet, apron!"

The line is out the door today, and Mama has no time to even glance in my direction.

In spite of the line, I run to the bathroom to wash my hands. They feel sticky, even though there's no more soap on them.

"Maya." Baba bangs on the door. "Turn that off already. Your hands are clean. Let's go!" I run out and slip on the hairnet, apron, and gloves. There's a tug at my insides to wash my hands again, but Babushka would probably break down the door.

Stomach tightening, I position myself behind the counter and force myself to smile at Mrs. Antonov, Kat's mom.

Just like her bestie, Mrs. Nelson, her eyes zoom straight to my hands. I wiggle my fingers in the air. "Just put on a fresh pair," I say too cheerily. *And nearly washed my skin off.*

"You really should hire more staff." She wipes a bead of sweat off her perfectly powdered face.

Be kind. "I am so sorry. I'll add two free pirozhki for your troubles." I make a show of placing two, perfectly browned, meat-filled pastries into a container.

"That's the least you can do," Mrs. Antonov mumbles, and she fans herself. She takes off her jacket, and I'm pleased to see small pit stains on her lilac blouse.

I grit my teeth and keep smiling, but my hands shake as I pack her items. I imagine germs traveling from my palms to the cracks in my skin, through the gloves.

Her foot taps the floor. Her fingers drum on the glass. *Tappity tap, tappity tap.* The beat pounds in my toes and my calves, and I close my eyes to block out the noise.

Mrs. Antonov takes a step back. "Are you all right, dear? I hope you're not coming down with something. Don't breathe too close to the food."

Would it be better if I breathed on your face?

Mrs. Antonov heaves a large, impatient sigh as I finish the last box and bring it to the register. My fingers tingle, and all I want to do is rip off the gloves and run to the sink.

Which I'm about to do, but Babushka shouts, "Number fifty-two!" My arms prickle, and my chest tightens.

"That's me!" Ms. Banta calls, jogging toward me.

Her hair is falling out of its clip, and her smile reveals lipstick-stained teeth.

"What can I get you?" I ask, trying to ignore the tingling.

She leans against the glass and spreads her hands out on the counter. "Everything looks so good," she says with a hollow laugh.

Her eyes dart from one item to the next, and she bites her lip.

"Why don't I just pack some of our favorites? Okay?" I say gently. When she doesn't respond, I add softly, "Three of everything."

She nods and rubs her hands along her knee-length coat. It hangs open to reveal a pilling gray sweater, which does not match her black pumps.

I count each pastry, appetizer, and entrée serving to make sure there are three. But Ms. Banta is not even looking. Her eyes dart to the exit as she tries to widen the space between herself and other customers—a hard thing to do, considering the line just keeps getting bigger and bigger.

"I'm almost done," I say.

"Please." Her voice is strained.

I rush to pack the boxes and run them over to Babushka. Ms. Banta slowly makes her way to the register. She's walking carefully, each step calculated to avoid anyone beside her.

I want to hover and protect her, but the line is growing. When Babushka calls number fifty-five, I'm back behind the counter and lose track of Ms. Banta.

"How can I help you?" I ask a teen in a floppy hat.

Suddenly, I see Ms. Banta from the corner of my eye, swaying, grabbing hold of the magazine stand to anchor herself, only to have it teeter and then fall to the floor, taking her with it. Her other hand shoots out to grab the next nearest thing, which happens to be the mahtroshkas, but they're not attached to anything either and clatter to the floor. Heads of the Simpson family roll around her. Ms. Banta pulls her arms around her knees as this week's *Otvet*, instructing readers to "WATCH! LISTEN! LEARN!," litters the tiled floor.

"I'm so sorry!" she keeps repeating. "So sorry!" She rocks back and forth, not trying to get up.

Babushka runs to her and whispers something, but Ms. Banta shakes her head. Customers bend down to help her, but she squirms away from them, thrusting her hands in front of her like a shield.

Ms. Banta chokes, "I just need to get out of here!"

She scrambles to her feet and tries to push through the crowd at the exit.

"That woman is crazy," Floppy Hat snickers, and that's when I see he has his phone out.

"Put that away," I hiss.

"No way. This is gold." He laughs and starts following her outside.

My face burns, and my stomach is tight as I elbow Floppy out of the way to reach Ms. Banta first. Not that I know what to do, but I don't want him there.

She's sitting on a bench, rocking back and forth. An ambulance pulls up. Two men get out and sit beside her, but she keeps rocking, moving her lips silently.

Finally, the EMTs help her stand, and she walks slowly to the ambulance but doesn't get in. The crowd thins. I stand by the door of The Russian Gourmet and will her to make eye contact so my face can let her know everything will be okay.

I stand for a long time.

"Maya, we need you in here," Mama says, tugging on my sleeve.

Ms. Banta needs me.

"Maya," Mama says louder.

Ms. Banta slowly walks away from the EMTs.

"Ms. Banta!" I call.

She turns, and I wish I had stayed silent. Her mouth forms a small O. Her eyes tear up, and her face reddens in shame. She quickly hurries down the street, and I follow my mother inside.

CHAPTER 18

> Were you there?

> ?

> ??

> ???

Val's texts blow up my phone as I sit at the kitchen table on Sunday evening. *Ping.* This time it's a video. I close my eyes, clench my fists, and try another calming strategy I read online—reciting the alphabet backward. *Z, Y, X.* Each letter comes to me with effort, as if I'm learning the alphabet for the first time. *Deep breaths. In*—*two, three, four. Out*—*two, three, four.* But the *whoosh* is loud today, and I give up.

"Put that thing away and help us make dinner," Babushka says. "Fried mashed potatoes, your favorite."

I switch the phone to vibrate, shove it into my pocket, and shuffle to the counter.

Mama and Babushka have a bucket of potatoes and three vegetable peelers ready. "Teamwork," Mama says, tousling my hair.

I pick up a potato and peeler and scrape the blade over the rough skin. Brown ribbons fall into the trash bin beside me. *Shwt, shwt, shwt. One, two, three.*

My phone vibrates against my hip, and I focus on scraping quickly, so I can grab another potato and just peel, peel, peel.

Each glistening, bare potato quiets the thoughts in my head. I reach into the bucket to begin more peeling. *Shwt, shwt, shwt. One, two, three.*

Bzzz. The vibration messes with my counting.

"When you're done," Babushka says, "chop the onions. Use those muscles." She winks and places a bowl of onions in front of me.

My phone buzzes again, and even though asking my question will bring the thoughts right back, I need to know. "Do you think Ms. Banta is okay?"

Babushka's scraping quickens. Mama grates.

"Look at you!" Babushka exclaims. "You finished all your potatoes. Here." She hands me a knife. "Get to chopping."

I try again. Louder. "Do you think Ms. Banta is okay?"

"Use the paper towels to squeeze the extra water from the onions so they'll crisp when we fry them," Mama says, handing me a roll of Bounty.

Bzzz.

I take a deep breath and keep chopping. Behind me, water bubbles as potatoes boil. Oil crackles, waiting for the onions. The buzzing of my phone travels from my hip to my stomach. Thoughts gather in the center of my forehead, then sprint to my temples, trying to get out.

Babushka peers into my bowl. "When you're done chopping, you can mash the first batch of the potatoes Mama and I boiled."

Tears pour down my face as the knife slices through onion layers. Mama hands me a steaming bowl of potatoes and the masher, and I drive it through the soft flesh.

"Don't forget the spices," Baba calls from the stove.

I generously sprinkle her special blend of salt, pepper, paprika, and garlic and keep mashing.

"Really get in there," Mama sings. "You want the flavors to mesh together."

My phone buzzes as the masher delves deeper and sweat piles on my forehead.

"Ms. Banta?" I try one more time.

Babushka lowers the flame on the stove, quieting the sizzle. She pours the onions into my potato bowl.

"I don't know, Maya," she answers, careful to keep her eyes on the mixture rather than on my face.

"You know what?" Mama adds, voice full of fake cheer. "I bet Ms. Banta would like fried mashed potatoes. I'll add it to her standing order."

I grab a large spoon and dig deep into the mush, making sure the onions are fully embedded in the potatoes.

"She seemed off all last week, too. Do you know what happened?" I ask.

Babushka and Mama exchange glances, but they ignore me.

"If you're done mixing," Mama says, "mash the next batch."

I slam the masher loudly against the bowl and smirk when she and Baba jump. "Do you know what happened?" I ask again, my voice rising.

"I don't, Maya," Babushka says. She pushes from her forearms as she plunges the masher into her bowl. She shakes her head. "I feel for her, I do, but you can't let your thoughts control you like that."

I tense. "It didn't seem like she could help it."

Mama checks on the onions and adds a new fried batch to her potatoes. "Your babushka isn't blaming her. It's just..."

My eyes water again, but this time it's not from the onions. "If she were stronger, she could have stopped it?" My breath catches. It's just like with the Google pages. Strong women don't give in to their feelings.

Babushka pulls me to her. "I know you really like her and are sad for her. Mama and I are, too. But—" She wipes my tears with the back of her hand.

"*Slozi goryu ne pomozhet,*" I whisper.

"That's right," Baba says. "And I'm sure Ms. Banta would like you to be strong for her."

Ms. Banta would understand my tears.

"I'm done," I say. I try to take the shakiness and weakness out of my voice—like Baba and Mama want.

Mama scans the kitchen to see if there's anything else I can do, but there isn't. "It will be okay," she says before I head upstairs.

In my room, I squeeze Pinkie and check my phone.

Did you watch??

There are at least ten texts from Val with a link to a video. Then, a series of question marks.

To watch feels like a betrayal, but how can I defend Ms. Banta if I don't? *You can do it. Be tough.* I click Play and immediately wish I hadn't.

Ms. Banta is huddled on the floor, eyes lost, body looking like it wants to fold into itself. She's shaking and mumbling something I can't make out. People crowd around, and Ms. Banta shakes her head violently and covers her face. Then she pushes herself up and wobbles out the door, like she's forgotten how to use her legs.

The comments section has over a hundred replies. **She's so crazy! This is a teacher at OUR school?? Take some meds, yo!** They go on and on. Maybe if I scroll far enough, I can find something positive, but I don't want to keep reading.

?? Val texts.

I stare at the question marks until they blur and become unrecognizable. What would I say? That it wasn't like that? That I get it? That I'm scared this could happen to me?

My fingers shake as I text. The text is light and breezy, and Val will never know it took me minutes to get the words out.

> **I was too busy helping Kat's mom 😒. Totally missed the whole thing! LOL**

I turn off my phone so there's no more buzzing and close my eyes. Images play behind my eyelids—of Ms. Banta, of Floppy Hat's smug face, of Baba wiping my tears. They repeat over and over like a bad film reel. I close my eyes tighter and try to find strength to push it all away.

CHAPTER 19

Monday morning, my feet drag across the gray tiled McKinley hallway like they're slogging through a swamp. Voices bounce off the lockers, walls, and ceiling like Ping-Pong balls. I've been thinking about Ms. Banta and wondering if she'll be in today, and the chorus of "sub" gives me my answer.

"You didn't answer my texts," Val says.

I fiddle with my locker combination, tugging until the lock finally unjams. "I did. I told you I didn't see anything."

Val stares at me, but I don't have anything else to say.

"It looked bad," she says.

I squeeze Pinkie and place all my attention on getting my books out of my backpack. I made myself watch the whole video three times to see if I remembered it all wrong or if it seemed worse than it was. But this time my brain didn't trick me. There was no mistaking Ms. Banta's rocking and hugging her knees and mumbling to herself. She looked like someone who broke. "I wouldn't know."

Val kneels down beside me and squeezes my hand. "Are you okay?"

"Just tired. My phone kept buzzing." I give her a pointed look. Her eyes widen, and I feel bad for taking this out on her.

She lets Kat and Lacey walk in front of us. I hear them mumbling before Lacey spins around. "Maya," she whispers my name. "Was it super scary?"

Kat and Lacey stare at me, like they can see my heart beating through the purple polka dots on my sweater. "I-I didn't see it."

Lacey narrows her eyes. "My mom almost didn't let me come to school today. She was afraid Ms. Banta would be here."

Val squeezes my hand again. I'd forgotten she was right next to me. "So? What if she was?"

Kat looks from Val, to me, to Lacey, confused, not getting why *we* don't get it. "Um, there's obviously something wrong with her. My mom thinks so, too. If she'd only been at the store a little longer, she could have seen *everything*."

My throat is dry. The hot-hot-hot is spreading, and I wonder if they see it. My fingers tingle. I narrow my eyes. "Your mom was in a rush to get out. Apparently, we're super slow."

Lacey puts her hands on her hips and glares at me. "How could *you* not have seen it?"

A man in a too-big gray suit walks to the doorway. "School is starting, ladies," he says. His squeaky voice is too small for his body.

Kat and Lacey don't move. Lacey taps her foot.

"Seriously, Lacey," Val says, moving in front of me. "Maya was working. How is she supposed to do *that* and see every crazy thing happening? Especially when she's dealing with people's crazy moms." She looks pointedly at Kat.

I flinch at the word *crazy* but know Val didn't mean it like that. And, anyway, she just saved me.

"Ladies!" the squeaky-voiced man calls again.

Kat gives me a clueless smile. "I'd be so mad if I missed it. *Everyone's* talking about it! Imagine if it happened here."

Lacey throws her hair over her shoulder, and the two of them walk into class.

"Thanks," I whisper to Val.

She shrugs and walks in front of me. She stuck up for me, but I can tell she doesn't believe me either. I squeeze Pinkie and shuffle to my seat.

Gray Suit walks to the front of the room. "I'm Mr. O.," he says, "and I will be subbing for Ms. Banta today, okay?"

"Ms. Banta lets us hang out," Barry says.

Mr. O. smiles and twirls his bushy mustache. "I somehow doubt that, but nice try." He sifts through the papers on Ms. Banta's desk. "It says here to begin with reading, okay?"

My stomach rumbles. The day starts with math. Reading is always in the afternoon.

Derek raises his hand. He has a rubber band positioned around his thumb and index finger, ready to shoot. "Can we just, like, start?"

Mr. O. smooths his mustache with his ring finger as he scans the paper again. "Grab your book and begin. Okay?" I'm starting to think that's what the *O* stands for.

Val slowly drags her chair to my desk, but her usual excitement about reading together isn't there. I make sure no one is within earshot, then lean in. "I *did* see, all right?"

She rubs her fingers across her thumbnail and bites her lip. "But why couldn't you just tell me?"

I shrug and squeeze Pinkie. "I didn't want to think about it, I guess." Even saying this one thing is like opening a portal. Images of Ms. Banta on the floor creep into my head. I shut my eyes tight.

Val's knee bumps mine. "It's okay," she says quietly. "I get it now."

I open my eyes and glance at her notebook. It has lots of doodles of Elsa and Anna. "Subject change," I say, grabbing her notebook. "Tell me about this masterpiece."

She giggles. "I've been dying to share my medley with you!" She flips pages to show me which songs she strung together. "My grandparents helped me. I think working together might push them to come see me onstage." She crosses her fingers.

Some kids are reading on the cushions. Others are in their seats reading, drawing, or writing notes. Mr. O. is at Ms. Banta's desk, a humongous coffee cup in front of him. His eyes are closed, and his chin is resting on his collarbone.

"Do you think Mr. O. will let us prep for the show?" Lacey whispers as she and Kat sidle up to us. I jump. Did they hear what I said about Ms. Banta?

As much as I'd like to ignore them, there's no way they're just being friendly. I give them my attention, hoping they'll get to their point and leave. "I hope so. We can all use more practice."

Lacey nods. "I'm working on some poems, and my mom says I should have music and props, too. I'm going to need time to put all that together."

"You can do it!" Kat says. "Being onstage is not really my thing, so I'll just be cheering everyone on."

"That's cool," I say.

We stare at each other awkwardly for a few more seconds before Kat nudges Lacey.

"Um," Lacey says, "you think your dad would let me go first?"

Finally! Now they can leave. "Sure," I say, relieved her request is so simple.

"Great," Lacey says. "Thanks." She starts to walk away, then turns back. "This school is totally lucky they got your dad before he became somebody."

I freeze, and Val narrows her eyes. "What's that supposed to mean?" she asks.

Lacey plays innocent and plucks lint off her sweater. "When he's famous, he'll be touring all over the place and won't be around much."

Kat tugs on Lacey's arm. "Let's go. I want to hear your poem again."

Lacey doesn't move. "Why does everyone look upset? I didn't mean anything. Just saying the school played it smart."

Kat pulls harder on Lacey's sleeve. "We're going to go," she says.

I see the gears moving in Lacey's head. This meanness might have cost her the spot she wants in the show. "Don't worry, Maya. Getting somewhere in this business takes *years*. I saw a whole reality show about it."

As they finally walk away, I hear Kat scolding Lacey in Russian, and Lacey shutting her down, saying she "fixed it" and to stop bothering her.

Val growls under her breath. "Don't listen to her," she whispers. "She doesn't know anything. Let's get back to the important stuff." She waves her songs in my face.

Mr. O.'s head flops backward, and he wakes up with a jump.

I take out my stylus and absently move it across my notepad. Dad wouldn't leave. Even if he got big, he could be plenty big in New York. It's the other thing Lacey said that's bothering me. Could it really take *years*? My plan doesn't have that long. Mama won't wait years for Dad to figure things out. And if Dad was still trying to make it as a comic even *one* year from now, Babushka would have even more proof his dreams are *choosh*. And where would that leave me? I'd still be fighting the *whoosh* with no end in sight.

Val bumps me with her hip. "It will all work out, Maya."

I give her a watery smile. There is only one way things can "work out." Artie needs to make up his mind ASAP, so Dad can get his dream, have his pick of spots, and come home.

CHAPTER 20

"I just want to know she's okay," I tell Mama on Saturday as she packs Ms. Banta's delivery. "Can I please take it to her?"

"I don't think that would be appropriate," Baba says before Mama can answer. "It's best if she just recovers by herself."

"All I'd be doing is dropping off food. How would that be a bother?" I motion for the order form so I can help her check off the items.

"It wouldn't," Mama says.

"Sarah! I thought we discussed this."

"*You* discussed this," Mama says, placing the last item into one of the bags. "And I did not agree."

"She doesn't need her head filled with—" Baba begins like I'm not even there. I don't need my head filled with what? Does she agree with Mrs. Nelson and Mrs. Antonov that Ms. Banta is dangerous?

I place a checkmark on the line labeled "compote" and shakily hand the paper back to Mama. She and Baba are having a silent conversation with their eyes. "What?" I ask.

"Ms. Banta has been asking to see you," Mama says. "She wants to talk and apologize." Baba storms out of the room, and Mama sighs. "I think it would be good for you. I know it's been a rough week."

So Mama picked up on that, too. We had a sea of revolving subs. After Mr. Sleepy, we got Ms. Chatty, who kept talking even when we were trying to work. Then, we got Mr. Coughy, the throat clearer, whose spit flew onto Barry's desk, missing mine by millimeters. And we haven't had one after-school talent show practice all week. Which has stalled things in my plan and made me extra jittery.

I run to get my coat. "When are we going?"

A half hour later, after Mama confirms with Ms. Banta, we pull into Ms. Banta's driveway. We walk up her red cobblestone walkway and stand under the porch awning as rain slithers down her path and pools over the drains by her garage.

"Come in," she says, flinging the door open and relieving Mama and me of The Russian Gourmet bags. "I just put on the teakettle."

I slip off my raincoat and boots and follow her into the kitchen. Mama does the same while Ms. Banta busies herself putting away the packages. She brings the cold items to her cheek before refrigerating them.

"Bathroom?" I ask, my hands begging to be washed before the tea.

"Down the hall to your left. I'll have treats out by the time you get back."

Her bathroom smells of familiar disinfectant, and I'm calmer even before I get back to the kitchen.

Three saucers and teaspoons sit atop lace place settings. One of those blue metal tins that holds a variety of cookies rests in the center of the table.

"Chamomile all right?" Ms. Banta asks when the teakettle whistles.

"Sure." I remember the anxiety website saying chamomile tea was good for calming nerves.

Mama squeezes my shoulder. "I'll be in the living room," she says, carrying her mug and cookies to the room beside us.

"How is everything?" Ms. Banta asks. Her hands shake slightly as she places the steaming mugs on the saucers.

I peek into the other room and see Mama engrossed in her book. "Okay . . . I guess. Yesterday's sub made the mistake of allowing everyone to play Silent Ball."

Ms. Banta groans. "It should be called Chaos Ball."

She sips her tea, then takes three chocolate cookies from the tin. I choose one with sprinkled sugar.

"Have you been doing work, too?" she asks.

I nod. "But each sub starts the day differently. I kind of hate it."

She frowns. "I'm sorry. That must be hard."

I shrug. "You'll be back Monday."

She takes another sip of her tea, taps her spoon three times on the mug—*tap, tap, tap*—then sets it back on the saucer. The return of patterns has to be a good sign.

"I'm not ready to go back," she says.

"But you seem fine," I say. Little sugar crystals fall off my cookie, and I gather them with my fingers and place them back on the cookie's surface.

"It does seem that way, doesn't it?" She smiles weakly and breaks her remaining two cookies into thirds and dips a piece into her tea. "It takes a lot to appear . . . fine."

I swirl my tea bag. Tears push at my eyes. "So there will be *another* sub on Monday?" Saying this seems selfish, especially after Ms. Banta admitted she's far from better, but going into school not knowing what to expect makes me feel like I'm on a roller coaster right before a big drop.

Ms. Banta's face falls. "I'm sorry, Maya. Until they know for sure how long I'll be out, they can't get a steady replacement. Let's hope the next one can stay a few days."

Whoosh.

"One more week, and then it's December break. That's not awful." I try to smile.

Tap, tap, tap. "That gives me three weeks to pull myself together."

The words remind me of something I read on the anxiety website: **Create a Goal**. Now it makes sense. Ms. Banta may feel off now, but she's using the next few weeks to get better so she can be well for the talent show. Why risk going back too early and ruin her chances for later? She'll be back after New Year's with plenty of time to help with rehearsals. I perk up. My phone pings, letting me know Dad is on his way. "I need to get going."

"Visit anytime, hon. It's always great to see you," Ms. Banta says as she walks Mama and me to the door. She runs back into the kitchen and returns with a ziplock baggie. "Cookies for the road."

"Thanks," I say as I put on my boots and coat.

"Thank you for having us," Mama says, warmly clasping Ms. Banta's outstretched hand.

"Get better," I say as we step onto her porch. "I can't wait for you to see my act."

Ms. Banta's smile wavers but returns quickly. "I'll be there jumping and waving."

As she shuts the door behind us, she knocks three times on the frame before locking it. Mama and I start walking and wave at Ms. Banta in the window. She grins, waves, and jumps up and down before closing the blinds.

CHAPTER 21

On my first day of December break, after scoring early spots, Dad spreads a late-night picnic of pizza and mozzarella sticks on the hardwood floor of his apartment.

After he sets down his slice and wipes the grease from his fingers with a crumpled napkin, I hand him my electronic notepad. Now that we're only three weeks away from the show, I'm starting to feel the pressure. Pressure to make sure I don't fall on my face onstage. Dad hasn't been to a practice in forever and hasn't been by the house since Chanukah, so I need to make this time with him count.

He swipes through my notes, laughing out loud as he reads. "You've written a lot! Not sure why I'm even here." He winks at me.

"Was the joke about Mrs. Nelson too much?"

Dad snorts. "What was it she said? Oh, yeah. How 'cute' my emceeing is. She deserves all that's coming to her." He tosses his napkin toward the trash. It falls right beside it.

"Dad, c'mon! If we lose business, Babushka will kill me."

Dad frowns. "True story."

"Right. So?"

"You're fine," he says. "I don't think it was clearly her. You made sure to say *some* customers. Read that joke about the cookies again."

I swipe back in my notepad. "*Look,*" I begin. "*I get not being familiar with Russian food, but one customer has questions about* everything *we sell. Yesterday, they pointed to a chocolate chip cookie and asked what those black things were. Really?*" I pause and make a face. "*I asked if they'd heard of Russian ant chips. My grandma doesn't let me help behind the counter anymore.*"

Dad slaps his knee. "Yes, I loved that. You have a flair for telling it, too."

"And it never really happened, but she's *always* nitpicking about what's in our food, and I *wish* I could say that."

"That's the key," he says. "When in doubt, tweak some things. Or, use your comedy to change history."

"If only!" I giggle. If comedy actually had that superpower, all my jokes would be about getting Dad and Mama back together.

I look back at my notes. "What about the one about Barry?"

"You made good changes to it about how *you* feel. You didn't reveal that he slobbers over your pencils or anything like that."

"Good point." I gnaw on my lip. "There's something else I've been thinking about."

He thumps his knuckles on his knees while he waits for me to continue.

"Shouldn't I write *more* about myself? I mean, I write about others around me and what I see. But don't comics also make fun of themselves? Like when you talk about the store, you talk about your feelings and stuff." The thing is, I don't want to share all *my* feelings and stuff. I don't want people whispering "Is she normal?"

He taps his toes on the floor. He seems especially jittery today, extra wired even when he was onstage earlier. Maybe he didn't get enough sleep yesterday. That happens a lot with him. "Let's see. You wrote about the store, the pencils." He snaps his fingers. "I forgot about the Lysol bit. That was really good. I'd heighten it also, like describe *more* smells, and then squeeze the Lysol in, know what I mean?"

I grab my notepad, then switch to my phone, just like he does. I jot down some ideas. "How's this? Ain't it funny how we all have smells we love? Fresh baked cookies, the ground after a downpour, pizza day at school . . . Lysol." Dad laughs, and I keep going. "Just hear me out." I wave my hands, like he does when he's trying to get the audience's attention. "You've had a long day at gym class, everyone's sweat is all over the place, school is germ city. Then, you sit down at your desk, take a deep breath, and mmm-mmm . . . disinfectant!"

Dad applauds. "Perfect. And that answers your last question. It's about you and pokes a little fun but doesn't reveal too much."

I like that. So, it's like the audience can get a peek into my head, but there's plenty that's just mine. "That makes sense."

He gives me a hug, and I snuggle into his shoulder. "You have a real knack for this, you know. Like the way you were able to rework that Lysol bit so quickly. It's not easy getting up onstage, Maya. You should feel really good about taking that risk."

I chew the inside of my cheek. "How is this so easy for you?"

Dad grimaces. "It's not!"

"But you look so relaxed onstage!"

"The moments leading up to the show are always hard." He rubs his chin, a faraway look in his eyes. "Worrying about whether I'll be funny, reworking my jokes, wondering if I reworked them enough. Always thinking ahead, always thinking too much."

I can so relate to never-ending thoughts. It makes me think he'd understand what Mama and Baba did not. It would be easier to explain with my Google pages, but I try anyway. "I overthink, too."

Dad moves closer to me. "About what?"

Noise starts behind my ears. Tingles prick at my toes. Is my overthinking the same as his? What if he brushes it all away, too? "A lot of things. School, this act, Barry, germs."

Dad strokes my hair. "If the act is too much for you, you don't have to do it. I'll still emcee."

What's with everyone assuming the act is the problem? The act is my whole plan—and it's working! "No! I like doing comedy with you. You, Mama, and I had so much fun." As I say this, I realize I actually do love crafting jokes, finding the right words, putting new spins on what I see each day. It makes me feel like a *real* comic, like Dad.

He looks relieved. "Are you just worried about getting up in front of everyone? That's totally normal. I told you I *still* worry about that." He pulls me to him.

If there was a way to do all the behind-the-scenes comic stuff without actually getting up onstage, I'd jump at it. But the stage part is not what I'm talking about. The hot-hot-hot has been a part of me since way before the show.

I wish I had the right words to explain my feelings to him. Even though the *whoosh* and tingles get worse, and my palms start sweating, I try one more time. "The germ thing is annoying."

Dad frowns. "What do you mean?"

I clasp my hands together, and my fingers climb on each other as if they're on a jungle gym. "I wash my hands a lot at our store, and Barry is so gross, I feel like I need to have sanitizer around all the time. He spits on the desk, you know." I pretend to gag. It feels good telling him this.

Dad laughs. "I would feel the same way. Not getting sick is so ingrained in us. I always bring wipes with me so I can wipe down the mic before I go on."

Wiping down the mic doesn't seem weird. "You just sanitize the mic? Because, for me, washing my hands—"

Dad waves his hand. "That's your baba's doing. I forgot how on edge I used to be at the store. Then, after working there the other week, it all came back. She's so worried about the customers and everything being perfect. I must have changed my gloves five times."

"I guess," I say. "But Barry—"

He hugs me. "Maya, I don't know *anyone* who wouldn't want to puke if someone kept spitting all over their desk."

My voice is a whisper when I say the next part. "Ms. Banta understood all my germ stuff."

He presses his lips together, and his eyes widen. He finally gets it. I can tell. There's someone else I can talk to about all this now. My heart beats faster.

"Oh Maya," he says, hugging me tighter. "Ms. Banta is going through a very hard time. I can totally understand why it would scare you. But that's not you."

And just like that I deflate. It's my fault for not waiting until I had the Google pages. I explained it all wrong.

"The thing is, Maya," he says as I lean my head on his shoulder, "you come from a long line of worriers. Mama and I gave you our sense of humor, and Baba added her work ethic. Then, we all gave you our worry genes, too. Unfortunately, you got stuck with the good *and* the bad."

There it is, *the long line of worriers*. It's like what Val was saying about everyone worrying and me making a big thing out of nothing. It's the same as when Mama and Baba said it's who we are. Maybe they're all right. Maybe what I should take away from this is that everyone worries, but they get through it. Dad even said he gets nervous *every time* he gets onstage.

"Why *do* you get nervous before each set if you know it's all going to work out?" I pull my knees to my chest.

Maybe his answer is the secret formula. He said he gets nervous each time, and each time it all ends up fine. That's like me getting nervous about Barry, but hasn't the worst happened? Didn't I get his germs on my fingers, and I'm still here? Band-Aids all over my hands from all the washing—but no infection . . . Yet.

He looks confused. "But I *don't* know it will be fine. Just because it worked out once doesn't mean it always will."

Just like with the elastics. Just because a cut didn't get infected one time doesn't mean it won't get infected another. Still . . . "But the odds are in your favor, right?"

Dad shrugs. "What can I say? Long line of worrying genes, remember? But," he pauses, "time heals all."

I force a smile. "Comedy equals tragedy plus time."

He raises his hand in a high five, and I slap it. "You got it. When I can, I spin things into a bit. Knowing I can turn my worry into something funny helps me handle it in the moment."

With that, he pulls up one of his jokes, and we workshop our material until it's time for bed. As I fall asleep, I think about how to weave my worries into something good, but I can't focus on anything except the bad images pushing at my eyelids. They spin like that tornado scene from *The Wizard of Oz*. I try the backward alphabet strategy, spending five seconds on each letter to give it time to overpower the bad stuff. By the time I get to E, the images have slowed down, and the letters have coated most of the worried spaces in my head. Not all, but enough so I can finally quiet the *whoosh* and get to sleep.

CHAPTER 22

Our first day back from winter break introduces yet another sub. Whispers bounce around the room until they stop sounding whispery.

"Is Ms. Banta coming back ever?"

"My mom says it's better if Ms. Banta doesn't come back. She really can't deal with people."

"My parents don't think she should come back either."

"Or mine."

"They're writing letters to the superintendent."

I put my head down on my desk and cover my ears. I wanted to call Ms. Banta over the break, but Mama said to let her be. Baba said she hadn't placed any orders, so maybe she was away. I shouldn't have listened. If I had gone over there, I'd have known she wouldn't be back today. Instead, I came to school with my hopes high, high, high only to have them nosedive to the dirty tiled floor.

"Class," the sub's voice filters in through my fingers, "I'm Ms. Franklin, and you're stuck with me for the next three days and next week at least."

At least? My stomach spasms, and the tingles shoot up my calves. Ms. Banta said they can't get a permanent sub until they know for sure how many days she'll be out. Does this mean she's not coming back? What about the talent show?

I raise my head and uncover my ears. Ms. Franklin looks younger than Mama, but streaks of gray hair frame her face. Green, dangly earrings, which match her green, beaded necklace, grace her neck. Her yellow dress swishes over her green suede boots as she walks around the room.

"I've read Ms. Banta's plans, and I'll do my best to follow them so there are no surprises," Ms. Franklin says.

Barry and a few others groan, but my tingles stop creeping.

She scans the paper in front of her. "I understand you have a talent show coming up? That seems fun! I was told you missed quite a few rehearsals, so I will help run practices while I'm here."

"Yes!" Lacey says. Some kids cheer and start changing seats.

Ms. Franklin raises her hand for silence. "I know you are all excited, but talent show prep is not on the agenda this week. Practices will start *next* week." She looks at the plans again. "Our first order of business is math."

Chairs scrape back to their original spots, and Ms. Franklin puts a math problem on the smart board. She's not Ms. Banta, but this could work. She's following Ms. Banta's directions, talent show rehearsals are back, I'll be okay. I can get back to my plan—which also means the hot-hot-hot can soon be gone-gone-gone. I move my hand to the pocket of my jumper and give Pinkie a squeeze.

Barry pushes his chair closer to mine, and I move away. He makes a big production of looking in his desk and shoving his stuff aside. "I hate math," he mumbles.

I ignore him and work on a problem.

"Ms. Franklin," he says, waving his hand in the air. Anything to waste time. "I don't have a pencil."

Ms. Franklin smiles. "I'm sure we can fix that. Can anyone lend—" she pauses to check the seating chart—"Barry a pencil?"

Barry didn't really bother me with the last two subs. For a second, I think he truly doesn't have a pencil. But then I see him reach into his desk and push his pencils far inside so no one else can see them.

Ms. Franklin's eyes flitter desperately around the room and land on me. No. I am *not* dealing with him today.

"Barry has pencils," I squeak out. "They're in his desk."

Ms. Franklin walks over to his desk, her heels clacking, her earrings jingling. "May I?" she asks.

Barry glares at me and pushes his chair back, allowing Ms. Franklin to peer into his desk.

She reaches far inside and pulls out two pencils with teeth marks.

"I must have missed those," he mumbles.

"I'm the same way," she says. "I forget what's in my closet all the time."

Ms. Franklin walks back to the smart board to go over a word problem, and everyone's eyes follow her. Barry starts writing, presses too hard, and his pencil point breaks. He does the same with the other pencil.

Pinkie presses against my thigh, and I keep my eyes on the smart board. Maybe if I ignore him, he'll bother someone else.

"Ms. Franklin"—Barry's hand shoots high in the air again—"my pencils broke."

Ms. Franklin purses her lips. She looks from Barry to the smart board. Her eye twitches. She clasps her hands together and forces a smile. I feel bad for her and throw a bright yellow pencil onto Barry's desk.

"Thanks, Maya," she says, looking relieved.

"Keep it," I tell Barry, who doesn't even say thank you.

He pushes his desk away from me and gets to work, a big smile on his face. He knows he won. I take a deep breath, hold it for four counts, and slowly let it out. It's over, so I should be relieved, but my insides still burn. The hot-hot-hot is back and creeps up my legs. My breathing quickens, and I try to breathe in and out, in and out. Will he act like this the whole time Ms. Franklin is here? I try to think of a way to make this moment into a bit, but I'm too on edge.

Barry doesn't look at me for the rest of the lesson, but I can't let go of what happened. I hate that he has my pencil. It messes up my rainbow set. Now, after my red and orange pencils, the rainbow skips right to green. RO G BIV.

When it's time to read, Val and I walk over to the cushions. The covers are half off and stained.

Val wrinkles her nose. "Let's just sit at our desks."

I take out my book, squeeze Pinkie, and try to match my shallow breaths to Val's slow, even ones.

She gently taps my wrist with her finger. "Ms. Banta would have known Barry was just being annoying," she says.

Hearing his name makes my eyes water. *It's just a pencil, Maya.*

"Don't worry," she says. "I'm sure Ms. Banta will be back soon." She gives me a hug.

A lump forms in my throat. I nod, not trusting myself to speak.

"Fifteen more minutes of reading time," Ms. Franklin says.

I give up on trying to focus on the words in my book and take out my pencils. Since the color pattern is off, I look for patterns in their points. I don't like that they're not even anymore. It makes the hot-hot-hot worse. I want the points to go from small to big. I scribble on my paper until there's a small difference in height with each one. I line them up, no longer focusing on the missing color Barry has. Instead, I look at their points, slowly increasing in size—just like mahtroshka dolls. My chest is still a little tight, but I feel the hot-hot-hot getting smaller, too. When reading ends, I quickly shove all but one pencil into my pencil case, out of Barry's reach.

Just three more days until my Barry-free weekend. Three more days until I see my dad at his next gig. And three more days until he can help me find something—anything—funny about the tragic way I'm feeling.

CHAPTER 23

The Bob's Bowling Bonanza sign flashes on and off, lighting up the packed parking lot. "You're performing *here*?" I ask, as Dad turns off the ignition. We passed a few farms on the way, and this area is a far cry from the city. "They have a stage?"

"Doubtful," Dad says with a shrug, "but it pays pretty well." Still, he doesn't look excited.

It reminds me of when he did the street fairs and farmers' markets. He didn't love it, but he called it "exposure." At least Mama was fine with me coming here.

"If I sign with Artie," Dad continues, finally getting out of the car, "I can get more paying gigs at better places, like colleges."

I don't really understand. "Isn't the goal to get better spots at comedy clubs?"

"That too, but the big comics fill their days with other gigs that will get them noticed. Like if you want to have your own Netflix special or appear on a late-night show, you need your name everywhere."

That sounds like he'll be around less, not more, if he signs with Artie. Did he just realize this or was this always the plan? I don't have a chance to ask, though, because he flings open the Bowling Bonanza door, and loud rock music fills the air. There are disco balls overhead that shower the floor and lanes in multicolored lights, and movies play on the large screens hanging down from the ceiling.

I survey the scene and try to figure out where he'll do his act. There are tables set up behind the lanes, but they're filled with snacks and drinks. There's also a video game room, but no one would see or hear him if he performed there. It's a pretty cool place and one I'd love to hang out in with Val, but it doesn't seem like an ideal spot for a stand-up gig. Then again, standing next to a horse with diarrhea didn't scream spotlight either, so this is a step up.

After speaking to the man renting out shoes, Dad motions for me to join him by the snack bar. The guy behind the counter gives Dad a red Solo cup with water, a chair, and a mic. The music disappears, but people's laughter and the toppling of pins fill the silence.

As Dad gets set up, so do I. I take out my phone and start recording. I know he's doing this weird gig to get seen, and what better way to be seen than by going viral? Comedians post short clips of their sets online all the time, so all he needs is one great joke with lots of laughter in the background. If people love the clip and he gets tons of likes, that will help put him on Artie's radar for sure.

"Hey folks," the Solo-cup guy says, "I'd like you to stomp those stylish bowling shoes and welcome James Greenspan." There's a smattering of applause, but nothing like the clubs Dad usually performs in.

"Thanks, Pete," Dad says as his voice rises above the balls barreling down the oiled lanes. "I'd like to welcome everyone to my bowling stand-up debut. This is how you know you've made it. They don't ask just anyone to perform in a bowling alley. Some comics get Madison Square Garden, but I'm all about the challenge."

Some people stop bowling and listen. A few laugh, others groan. But then everyone resumes playing again. Pete makes trips back to the counter in between cleaning out the soda machines and fryer. I stop the video and listen for a good spot to restart.

He starts in on some crowd work, where he walks past different groups, asking questions, trying to get them involved in his act.

"Is this your typical Saturday night?" he asks an older couple.

The white-haired man hugs the woman beside him and says, "It's our forty-second wedding anniversary today."

People cheer. Dad whistles. "Forty-two years, wow. And you're celebrating *here*?"

"Hey!" Pete yells.

"Let me backtrack," Dad says. "You're celebrating HERE! Good for you!"

A guy in a tank top and torn shorts gets a strike, and the cheers from his group drown out Dad's punch line. A mom grabs her toddler and runs past my dad to the bathroom as her kid leaves a trail of throw-up. "I'm not for everyone," he jokes, pausing for two giggles.

The older man's wife adjusts her pink headband over her salt-and-pepper hair. "They're giving us a free dinner."

"That's a good deal. They didn't give *me* a free dinner."

That wasn't bad, but not totally viral-worthy. I start another recording, hoping to get one truly funny clip.

But it doesn't come. He barely gets any laughs, but he keeps trying anyway. Because he has to, and it's what he's been paid to do. Not because it makes him *pop, pop, pop*. I stop recording and shove the phone into my pocket. After thirty minutes, most people stop listening altogether. Teens shout to bring back the music. Even Pete's opened a magazine. It's so wrong. Dad's doing his best. Why did they even invite him? My eyes water. What if Artie had seen a show like this? Would he have blamed Dad? It's unfair how much of his dream is not in his control.

"Well, that's my time," Dad finally says an hour later. "Thanks for being . . . an audience. I'm gonna split."

There's some applause, and I busy myself at the claw machine while he waits to get paid.

"C'mon, kiddo," he says, putting his arm around me.

He bangs the steering wheel when we get to the car. Then, he laughs. "That was awful, huh?"

I look out the window and try to think of something positive, because the truth is, it *was* awful. "You tried."

He puts the car in reverse, and we peel out of Bob's. I can see his eyes now, and they're dark and blank. I get up the courage to ask what I've been thinking all night.

"You want more gigs like *this*?"

He lets out a deep breath. "Gotta pay my dues."

"Haven't you been paying them for years?" I mean, isn't that why he's not living with us anymore?

"Not really," he says. "While the up-and-coming comics were taking anything available, I was working on my law degree and doing spots when I could. But I wasn't totally happy with the law stuff, and each time I'd finish a spot, I'd want to do another. And then there was this shore trip—"

"The apricots," I say as things start clicking.

He looks confused, but then nods. "Right, the apricots. Your mom went to find these special apricots, and I went to see an old comic friend. He was doing so many great things. He was auditioning for a TV pilot in Los Angeles, and he was going to have a showcase in—"

"You wanted to be on TV?" My head is spinning. California is so far away. That's not my plan. My palms are sweating. The lump in my chest gets bigger, and I try to swallow.

"Not specifically, but it reminded me that my dream career was comedy, not law. I made a whole plan of how to make that dream happen without thinking about how it would impact your mom's dream with The Russian Gourmet. And here we are."

"Here" is leaving a place that does not resemble a comedy club at all. What happened between him and Mama makes more sense now—but also less. I still don't understand why he thinks his dream and Mama's dream can't overlap. Hasn't he been seeing that they can mesh? These last few weeks he's been able to help with the show *and* work at the store. I try to smush all the information together, like when you try to complete a puzzle and shove pieces into each other even when they don't fit. "And Artie will help how?"

Dad's face shows surprise. "What do you mean?"

The *whoosh* is back in full force. I close my eyes to quiet it. "You said he can get you more paying gigs. But another time you said you'd have more time for us and would need *less* nighttime spots."

Dad keeps one hand on the steering wheel and hugs me with the other. "Both of those are true. He can get me more gigs with better time slots. If my name gets out there, I could do slots that start at eight or nine instead of midnight, or I could even have a standing gig at *one* club."

I nod. This makes sense. The late-night spots were Mama's biggest issue. Artie seems like he'll take care of that. I take a deep breath in and slowly let it out.

Dad gives my shoulder a squeeze. "It will be great, Maya, you'll see."

I crack the window so the highway sounds drown out the *whoosh*, then move as close to Dad as my seat belt will allow.

CHAPTER 24

On Wednesday after talent show practice, I walk into The Russian Gourmet—Dadless. Baba shakes her head, clucks her tongue, and mumbles something about empty promises.

Not gonna lie. When Dad told me he couldn't make it, I was annoyed at first, too. But then I realized I could use his not being here to my advantage. Ready to regroup after my viral video failure, I catch Mama by herself before Baba hounds me about getting to work.

"Our sub, Ms. Franklin, wants to meet all the parents at the next rehearsal." I bounce on my toes, feeling up, up, up about this part of my plan. Even though it's a lie, it's a tiny one and won't hurt anyone.

Mama looks distracted as she finishes shelving the salads. "The next one? We have a lot of order pickups. Isn't it enough that your dad is there?"

I expected her to say this and pretend to look worried. "I tried to tell her, but—"

Mama closes the glass case. "It's fine. I'll figure it out." Her face softens, and she taps me gently on the nose with her index finger. "It will give me the chance to see a special preview, too!"

Yes! "Thanks so much!" I throw my arms around her waist. She'll be so impressed with how dedicated Dad has been to the show and how far I've come with my act. And then he'll come to the store after and blam! Two dreams for the price of one.

"I'm next!" Mrs. Nelson calls.

I slip on a new pair of gloves and jump into action. "How may I help you?"

She moves closer to the case and uses her fingers to tap out a tune on the glass. "I have no idea. It's been a day, know what I mean?" She exhales loudly.

"Believe it or not, I do." This is the first time she's not treating me like a speck on her shoe, and it makes me think she's up to something. I yellow light it until I know what that something is. "Stocking up on Lacey's favorites?"

"She likes the borscht, dumplings, chicken. Just pack up fifty dollars' worth of stuff. I'll have it for two days." She unbuttons her coat and fans herself.

"Too hot in here?" I say, even though I know the temperature is just fine.

Mrs. Nelson shrugs. "A little."

"Sorry about that. We'll do better."

She smiles. "Maybe it's me."

Something is definitely off.

She looks around the store, her eyes flitting to the cameras in the corners. Then, she types something into her phone. If she's casing the place, she should be less obvious.

I close the containers tightly, placing tape around the lids to make sure they don't open. "Anything else?"

She takes something out of her pocket and leans in. "Actually, there is," she says in Russian. "Do you understand what I'm saying? Lacey says you don't speak too well."

I bristle. "I understand fine," I tell her in Russian.

"We're creating a petition to present to the board of education expressing our concerns about Ms. Banta," she whispers.

My heart beats quickly. My fingers form fists. "What concerns?"

She looks annoyed. "You were there. That woman is not well and should not come back."

My voice rises. "Why not?"

Baba and Mama are immediately at my side.

"What's the problem?" Baba says in Russian.

Mrs. Nelson smooths her coat. "I was just trying to explain to your granddaughter the importance of keeping our schools safe. But I'm afraid with her poor Russian, she had trouble understanding."

"I understood perfectly," I say too loudly in English. Customers stop their browsing and look in our direction.

"So sorry," Mama says to Mrs. Nelson. "I'll take it from here."

"But Mama—"

Mama gives me a tight-lipped smile. "It's fine, Maya. Help someone else."

I clench my fists tighter as Baba takes all of Mrs. Nelson's food to the counter, and Mama apologizes for my behavior. Mrs. Nelson points at the cameras.

My throat tightens, and I run to the bathroom. I cover my hands in soap so it looks like I'm wearing white gloves, and scrub my nails against my palms. I rinse off the suds and repeat. My hands feel sticky, like the soap is still on them. Rinse and repeat again.

There's a line waiting for me when I get back. I quickly put on new gloves and motion the customers forward, making a point of speaking Russian to each one, no matter how broken my words sound. Just to prove that I completely understand Mrs. Nelson's game—and I won't let her win.

CHAPTER 25

Arkham Comedy Club's gray exterior stretches high into the sky, with statues of rams and children sticking out from the stone. The building is old and weathered, and the children look creepy, with pieces of their faces chipped and discolored. There's even a gated entrance, like in the Arkham Asylum in Batman movies. It's the exact type of place Gotham's criminals would visit on a lightning-filled night.

Two lit-up marquees boast names of new, big-time comedians who'll be opening this weekend, and I watch my dad's face as we stand beneath the headliners' names on Saturday night.

"Those guys started when I did," he says, thrusting his hands into his pockets. He stares at the signs and shakes his head.

I want to cheer him up by saying something supportive, but it's been a month since he'd last performed for Artie and he told Dad he'd be in touch.

I try anyway. "It's going to be your turn soon. I can feel it."

Dad forces a smile. "You can, can you?"

"Yup! I bet Artie just doesn't want to distract you from your massive talent show gig."

Dad laughs for real now. "That must be it."

He squares his shoulders and tries to get showtime ready. As we walk in, other comics wave to him and call out his name, and he does the same. Some just give friendly nods.

We walk into the room where he'll be performing, which looks similar to all other club rooms. Same red walls with brown wooden chairs and tables, same stained carpeting. Tons of overhead lights. It's like all clubs had the same decorator. A spotlight shines on the empty stage, illuminating a large drawing showing the New York City skyline. I choose a chair in the back—like always. I like knowing that some things are the same no matter where Dad and I end up.

The overhead lights dim, and the emcee gets onstage to warm up the crowd. He introduces Dad, but just as he's about to get onstage, he runs over to me, face panicked.

"The *kapow*," he whispers.

"Uh, James Greenspan?" the emcee calls into the audience. "Comics, am I right?" His voice has an edge to it.

I quickly bring my fist to meet Dad's, and then we splay our fingers, his wedding ring glinting in the dim light. *"Kapow!"* we say at the same time. His face lights up like it always does before he takes the stage, and I breathe a sigh of relief when I see no trace of blahness in his eyes, like at the bowling alley. I lean back in my chair, the butterflies in my stomach resting their wings, and Dad grabs the mic. "Comics!" he says to the laughing audience. "We have issues."

The emcee laughs and shakes his head, and Dad dives into his bits.

It's at gigs like this—not the bowling bummer—that I can see the real him onstage. When people grab each other, like they're about to fall over, Dad literally bounces.

I imagine myself commanding the talent show, passing the mic from hand to hand. In my head, I'm beaming at the audience, pausing at all the right spots. Ms. Banta, Mama, Dad, and Baba jump to their feet, their faces bursting with pride.

All too soon, Dad is twirling the cord around his fingers and putting the mic back in the stand.

"Thank you all!" he says. "You've been great!"

The audience cheers. I'm already standing by the time he reaches me, and he lifts me onto his shoulders and gallops outside.

He hasn't done that since I was five, and I'm cracking up when he puts me down on the sidewalk.

"We killed that one," he says.

It's always "we," like I'm his good-luck charm. The word is like ice cream on a hot day, flowing through me and making everything okay. "They were really into it." I give him a hug.

He waves his arms as he talks. "The air was crackling. You heard it, right?"

He's walking fast, and I run to catch up. I didn't hear any crackling, but I feel this *pop, pop, popping* coming off him now. I wish Mama could be here, too. His energy is so big right now, even Baba would be pulled under.

Then, he stops so quickly, I almost bump into him. He pulls his phone from his pocket and swipes Accept on a call.

"Hello! So great to hear from you," he says. Then he mouths *Artie*, and we duck into a hotel lobby.

His voice is calm and even, but his eyes are wide. "That's terrific! Can you text me the address?"

Does he want Dad to sign up for another spot? Hasn't he seen enough?

"Noon tomorrow. Got it," Dad says, pacing and running his hand through his hair. Then after another beat, he finally says, "Thanks, man. I really appreciate this."

He hangs up and grabs my hand, and we run outside again. We link arms and spin around like we're dancing the hora at a Bar Mitzvah.

"Watch it!" someone shouts, but we just laugh, not caring that we're seconds away from ramming into someone.

He wouldn't be this happy if he had to audition again. "It's done?" I squeal.

"We're finalizing everything tomorrow," Dad crows. "It's happening!"

And it's like fireworks exploding. I swear I hear a crackle in the air.

"It's happening!" I shout back.

I take a photo of him in front of the marquee, and we laugh as we Photoshop his name in.

"Good thing you agreed to emcee the talent show before you got big, or they'd have to pay you mega bucks!" I say.

"Eh," he says, eyes twinkling, "I'd give them a deal since I know one of its stars."

"We have to celebrate!" I say.

He nods in agreement. "Sundaes. Every topping you want."

"The star treatment is beginning. I can get used to this."

We stop at a supermarket and throw three different pints of ice cream into the cart. They're the fancy kinds with cherries and caramel and chocolate bits and funky names like Merry Cherry and Caramel Karma.

"No boring vanilla and strawberry for us," Dad says, tossing chocolate syrup into the cart.

"No store-brand syrup for us," I add, swapping out the plain syrup for the kind that hardens and creates a candy shell.

I grab the marshmallows with chocolate inside, and Dad tosses mini marshmallows on top of them. "We get choices now," he says.

"That's how the Greenspans roll." I load my arms with a jar of maraschino cherries, marshmallow fluff, cookies, and sprinkles, and Dad gets the Cool Whip and whipped cream.

"Choices!" he calls across the aisle.

I stand on the back of the cart—something I haven't done since I was little—and Dad zooms to checkout. Soon we're back outside, arms loaded with more choices than we know what to do with.

CHAPTER 26

"It's all about making choices," Dad tells Val at Tues-day's after-school rehearsal in the auditorium. "There's limited time. You have to choose the Disney songs you connect with most."

Val's face grows serious. "Maybe the ones Joey and my grandparents like the best. I have my toes and fingers crossed they'll come." She gives Dad a small smile. "I'll even learn to cross my eyes if that will help."

Dad pats her on the shoulder. "I'll do the same." He winks at her, and Val gives him a quick hug before running back to one of the folding seats in the center of the room beside Ms. Franklin.

"Maya?" he says.

I walk slowly to the stage and take the mic out of its stand, like I've seen him do. I work on pacing back and forth like he does, but I'm thinking so hard about looking at the audience and where to walk, I can't focus on what I want to say. Where's the Maya that I kept picturing killing it onstage? Oh yeah. She's imaginary.

I sit on the stage, flustered. "It's too hard to do the jokes and the moves at the same time."

"What moves?"

I peek at the audience and am relieved Mama isn't here yet. I don't want her seeing me frazzled. "You know, the pacing, grabbing the mic, putting it back, all the little things you do."

He rubs his chin with his fingers. "I've never paid attention to what I do. Everyone does what's right for them. For example, some terrific comedians sit on a chair the whole time. Do you want to try that?"

I drag a chair from behind the curtain and place it at the center of the stage. I take the mic and look out at the seats in front of me. Right now, only twenty are filled, and everyone is focusing on their own thing. This will be much scarier the day of the show. I clear my throat and try a few lines from my set.

"Ain't it funny what celebrities can get away with and still be 'normal'? One has a coat hanger collection, and another collects hair. But, when I want to organize the ABC gum stuck to the bottom of my desk by size and color, it's all 'That's so disgusting, Maya!'"

Barry's face turns red, but then he laughs loudly and stops working on the set design to listen to more. At least he knows a good joke when he hears one.

Dad laughs, too, and gives me a thumbs-up.

I wait for the tingles and hot-hot-hot, but they don't seem up for an appearance. I can't believe it. Weeks ago, just thinking about my fingers smushed in Barry's slimy gum would send me into a handwashing frenzy. Now I can laugh about it. It's just like Dad said: Comedy equals tragedy plus time.

"Now, try it again and see if you want to practice standing this time. If it doesn't work, don't worry about it."

I retell the gum joke, and even Kat giggles. Knowing what I'm going to say and how I'll deliver it makes me more confident and in control.

"There you go! You got it!" Dad says, punching his fist in the air. "Lacey? You're up."

I get off the stage as Lacey walks on, and that's when I see Mama in the audience.

I run to her and give her a big hug. "When did you get here?"

"During your gum joke. You looked so natural up there." She ruffles my hair and pulls me to her. "Don't you go getting a big manager, too."

"I still have a few years before that happens." I wink at her. "But how awesome is it about Dad?" He called her after we got the ice cream, and I heard her scream through the phone.

"It's really hard to get into this business when you're older, and I'm very proud of him." She looks around. "Where's Ms. Franklin, so I can tell her I'm here?"

I don't see her at her seat. Lucky for me. "I think she went to the bathroom or something." I hook my arm through Mama's. "When Dad comes to help at the store later today, you should totally tell him you're proud of him."

Onstage, Lacey argues with Dad's advice about how to make the most out of her music and poems. But when he reminds her that she has a big responsibility as the first act, she stops fighting him.

"He said he wants to help today?" Mama says.

"I'm sure he will." He told me he was going to change his spots to make today work.

When everyone has had their turn onstage, Dad jogs up to us and hugs both Mama and me.

"Maya did great," Mama says, pulling out of Dad's hug, "and it was cool watching you give everyone pointers."

Dad blushes. "Yeah, well, I'm a big deal now."

She laughs. "Which is why I was surprised Ms. Franklin needed to see me, too. Let me make my appearance."

But as Mama starts walking her way, Ms. Franklin beats her to it. "Lovely to meet you," Ms. Franklin says to Mama. "You are one talented family!"

Mama smiles. "We do our best."

Ms. Franklin checks her watch. "I'm sorry I can't chat more, but I look forward to seeing you at our show!"

She speeds away, and Mama looks both relieved and confused.

I shrug. "Something must have come up." I link arms with Mama and Dad, and the three of us walk out together, our feet in step.

Once we're at the car, Dad leans in to hug me goodbye.

"You're not helping at the store today?" I ask. He didn't help last time either. Or the time before that. What else could he have meant when he said he would make today "work"?

Dad's eyebrows knit together in confusion. "I moved things around to help with the acts, but I have spots in two hours."

"It was great you could assist the kids today," Mama tells Dad. She sounds so . . . formal, and her voice is tight.

"Sarah, I didn't know you needed me at the store."

Mama waves his worry away. "Your help is always welcome, but it's all good. I'll see you this weekend?"

Dad bristles at that. "Why wouldn't you?"

"Just checking." Mama puts her arm around my shoulders.

Dad's jaw tightens. "We're all set." He gives me one more hug, and Mama and I walk one way and Dad the other.

Is she upset because I got her hopes up about Dad and the store? I was trying to bring them together, but maybe I made things worse. Right now, it looks like she came to support *our* dreams, but Dad can't do the same back. I need to fix it. "He just got signed," I say when we get in the car. "Soon, he'll have better gigs and be at the store more, but it takes time."

Mama sighs. "Buckle up, Maya." She looks in her rearview mirror, and a tear falls down her cheek. She quickly wipes it away. She obviously still cares about him, so why can't she try being positive?

"You'll see," I say, grabbing the seat belt.

Mama shakes her head. "He has his own life, Maya."

And I have nothing to say back, because I thought it was finally clear that we could all share *one* life.

CHAPTER 27

"I need to tell you something, Maya," Dad says on Saturday as we sit at one of the tables in the Liberty Comedy Club. A drawing of buildings hangs on the brick wall behind the dimly lit stage. The words *Liberty Comedy Club* are written in blue cursive across the black buildings. "Next week—"

"Ah, your smaller half," Luke, the club's host interrupts, noticing us in the corner. "Did your dad mention the Kids' Comedy Showcase I'm putting together?" He adjusts the elastic on his oversize man bun.

"I think he was just about to." I look at my dad, but he's not listening. He's back on his phone, perfecting his jokes.

Luke lifts his black-rimmed glasses and winks. "Keep me posted."

"Was the showcase what you wanted to talk about?" I ask Dad when Luke walks away.

"One of the things," he says, still looking at his phone. "You'd be great!"

I bite my lip. "I love the idea of us workshopping jokes together, and last week's rehearsal showed me I can stand on the stage without fainting, but a big crowd of random people? I don't know . . ." Really, I *do* know. As much as I like writing jokes and making people laugh, a random showcase would be too much for me. But he's into the idea, so I don't want to disappoint him just yet.

"It would definitely be fun," he says, but he seems distracted, probably because he has to be onstage soon. "No pressure." He goes back to his phone.

"Tonight's act?" I ask, leaning over.

"Yes, but I'm not sure about some of these. Should I keep doing the Russian store bit?"

That's one of his better ones, but whenever I think about it, all I can picture is Ms. Banta huddling in a corner and those awful comments beneath the video. And him not working there this week. "Something else may be better." I pick at the ripped red vinyl on the chairs.

"You're right," he says, frowning. "I think it's gotten stale."

"Yeah, maybe."

"How about something about all my weird jobs?" He types ideas into his phone.

I nod. "Like that bit you have about working for the company that sold toilets but didn't give their employees bathroom breaks?"

He snaps his fingers and hugs me. His goatee tickles my cheek. "You're the best!"

So much has changed in a week. Soon, his name will be on the front marquee for real, not just because of fancy editing skills.

"Maya, listen," he starts, but he's interrupted by a group of giggling women making their way into the theater. They're purposely loud, like when Kat and Lacey laugh at something "private" but keep looking around for a reaction.

One is a redhead, another a brunette, and the third has caramel highlights in her dark hair. Their metallic, sequined tops shimmer each time they pass under an overhead light. Their knee-length black skirts *swish* as they walk, and their high black boots make clicking noises on the tiled floor. I wish this club had stained carpeting to match its red walls like in all the other places my dad performs.

Suddenly, they're beside us. Dad squirms and puts his arm around me, pulling me to him. To protect me or himself?

"And here's the man we came to see!" squeals the woman with the highlights. Up close, the women look young. Way younger than Mama.

A grimace replaces Dad's earlier smile. "I didn't know you were coming."

"I wanted to surprise you," Highlights says. She puts her hand on his, but Dad snatches it away.

I push myself into the crook of Dad's arm, wanting to disappear.

The hot-hot-hot starts. My stomach clenches. The *whoosh*, which has been pretty quiet this week, creeps in from the crevices where it's been sleeping. I bring my knees to my chest. *I'm tiny. I'm invisible.*

Dad types something into his phone, and Luke magically appears.

"Ladies," he says smoothly. "Can I show you to a table? We're about to get started."

"James," Highlights begins, her voice gaining volume, but Luke whispers something in her ear, and she moves slowly forward. He seats her group at a table on the far right and steps into her line of vision when she turns around.

I'm tiny. I'm invisible.

Luke gives Dad a thumbs-up, and Dad raises his fist to mine for the *kapow*. I go through the motions because I know he needs it, but it barely registers when he walks to the stage. Sweat gathers at the back of my knees, and I close my eyes and focus on breathing. I hear Dad's voice, but I can't pay attention, and practice slow inhales and exhales.

A thought creeps into my head, and I open my eyes and search the audience. They zero in on Highlights. Even when she whispers to her friends, her gaze doesn't leave the stage. Dad faces forward, his head not moving in her direction at all. Is *she* what he's been trying to tell me? It can't be. My parents were weird with each other at the talent show practice, but Mama was the first person he called when he found out about Artie.

The breathing isn't working, so I look past Dad and focus on the blue cursive letters. The colors pop up, like they're 3D, and I stare at them until they're blurry like in those Magic Eye images. Just as it's starting to help, and I feel my breathing slow, the audience applauds.

Dad waves goodbye and sprints to my side.

"We're outta here," he says, barely waiting for me to get out of the chair.

I run to catch up to him, and we speed past the red walls and the famous faces that line them.

"James!" Highlights shouts, and Dad quickens his step.

"Maybe you should say goodbye to her," I whisper.

"No."

The chime of his phone follows us as we rush into the chilly night.

"Stop," I gasp, hands on my knees.

The cold air, mixed with the sweat beading inside my clothes, makes me feel colder. Dad puts his hand on my shoulder and steers me to a bench. I sit and close my eyes.

"Maya," he says, putting his hand on my arm, "are you okay? I'm so sorry about that." No, I'm not okay. Not only is it hard to breathe, but images of Highlights flash behind my eyelids.

"Maya?" His voice is panicked.

"Give me a minute." I slowly recite the alphabet backward in my head. Concentrating on the letter order helps me block out the other thoughts. By *M*, I'm able to open my eyes again.

"Do you want to talk?" he asks.

I wouldn't even know where to start. Should we talk about a random woman who touched his hand? Should I talk about struggling with my breathing? His face is still so worried. I'm supposed to *get* him, not worry him. Talking about everything would worry both of us a lot more. It's better to just sit quietly than risk the *whoosh* getting louder.

"I planned on taking you to the High Line tonight. It's a really neat place to walk," Dad says, watching me carefully. "You would have liked it."

It's only six o'clock. It's High Line or dinner, and I'm not ready to eat dinner. The thought of looking at him across the table while he tries to tell me whatever it is he's not been able to say makes me feel sick. "So let's go."

"Really?" he says. "Are you sure?"

I shrug. "Why not?"

There's an actual bounce to his step, like he'd skip to the High Line if he could. And even though the chime of his phone reminds me of the club scene we just left behind, seeing his bounce and knowing I did that makes me feel like we're a team again. "I love it there. Watching the people, lights, and cars from above always helps me clear my head."

We walk two blocks, up flights of concrete stairs, and it's as if we're in a new world. Like Narnia or some magical place not yet discovered. Old railroad tracks, now serving as home to a garden, bookend a stone walking path. Tiny lights guide our way in the darkness. I'm able to really breathe here. The *whoosh* and tingles are still there, but they've retreated to their corners, rather than being front and center.

"I want to show you my favorite spot," Dad says. He doesn't look worried anymore. The High Line is his backward alphabet.

We stop beside an overlook with rows of metal bleachers and head to the clear, plastic partition beneath them. As we stare at the world below, I can make out the exterior of the Liberty Comedy Club—its blue neon sign only a blurry speck. Multicolored lights flash from the cars and traffic signals, and I focus on the ribbons of red, green, and yellow and flashes of white zooming by.

"It's different from up here, isn't it?" Dad murmurs. "You feel . . . like your worries don't matter. I imagine everything leaving my head, traveling down, and disappearing into the night rainbow."

"The night rainbow," I whisper. "I like that."

I expect my words to be lost in the honking and shouts beneath us, but they're not. It's like we're in two separate realms—the pedestrians and drivers in their world, and us in ours. I know we're up here for a reason, for him to tell me something that I don't want to hear, but for a few minutes, I pretend we're just here for the peace and the sights.

Soon the silence between us is too thick. I ready myself for the louder *whoosh* and pull off the Band-Aid. "That thing you wanted to talk about? Is it about that woman?"

He looks surprised. "What woman?"

I roll my eyes. "C'mon, Dad. I'm not blind. The one at the club."

He leans on the railing. "I'm really sorry. I didn't know she was coming."

Maybe she's no one. Maybe she's just helping him with his act . . . like Mama used to do.

The cars and people rush at me. Millions of lights force their way into my brain. "Is she your girlfriend?" I can barely get the words out. I don't even know what I'll do if the answer is yes.

Dad snorts. "Not at all."

"She seemed to like you."

He takes a deep breath. His phone chimes. He looks at it quickly and shoves it into his pocket. I bet it's her.

"I didn't handle that situation well," he says finally. "You don't need to worry about her. Promise."

My insides relax, the bubble getting smaller again. She's no one. Not at all.

I think of Mama's tears in the car. Maybe Dad just needs to know she still cares about him.

"I know Mama misses you," I say.

He buries his hands in his pockets. "I miss her, too. And you."

I put my arm on his. "You said this lady wasn't important. So, when you come over next week after the rehearsals, you and Mama—"

"Maya, I can't," he says.

Nope. That doesn't work. I start to ramble. "Well, yeah, Baba may be annoyed, but when she sees you're serious about helping, it will all be fine—"

"Maya," he interrupts. "That's—"

The blob in my stomach returns. "No," I say forcefully. "Artie is your manager now. You're getting what you wanted. No more last-minute gigs. You can be around more."

The blob pushes at my sides. I tap my thighs with my fists and feel the tears coming. I don't wipe them away.

"Maya, sweetie," he says, guiding me to the bleachers beside us. His face is both pained and confused. "I can't be at the dress rehearsals. I have a gig in Canada next week."

"But you've been helping me! We've been doing this together. Now you won't even be at the show?"

"Of course I'll be at the show!" he says. "And I'll still emcee it. I'd never let you down like that. I just can't be at the final dress rehearsals."

"What if you get an amazing gig the week of the show?" I snap.

He shakes his head. "I already told Artie I can't do anything that will interfere with that."

The wind blows, and I hug myself. "But you were going to be around next week," I say weakly. I had a plan. And Mama is already annoyed he hasn't been helping at the store like she thought he would. Like *I* said he would. This week was going to fix all that. Everything was going to go back to how it used to be, and the *whoosh* would take the first flight back to where it came from.

He blows on his hands. "Your mom and grandma can take care of the shop. It will be fine."

Well, of course they can take care of The Russian Gourmet. They always do. But I needed them to see that Dad could put them first, too.

"You promise you'll be at the show?" My voice shakes.

He pulls me into a big bear hug. His arms are so strong, I will them to push the hot-hot-hot away. I wish they were magic just like this place pretends to be.

"Maya, I wouldn't miss it for anything. Cross my heart. And even when I'm in Canada, I will video chat with you and text—anything you need to work out the last bits of your act. I'll tell Mama to work with you, too." He hugs me tighter.

I take a jagged breath. I imagine bits of my plan crashing to the ground below. But it's not totally hopeless, right? Mama and Baba will still be at the show, and they'll see how perfectly everything came together. How *Dad* helped put it all together. That could happen. That *will* happen. It *has* to.

I wipe my runny nose on his jacket.

"I guess I deserve that," he says, a smile in his voice.

I laugh. "That's your punishment."

"I accept." Dad takes my hand. "Ready to get some grub?"

His phone pings again, and I take my hand away.

"Let's just stay in Narnia a little longer," I say.

CHAPTER 28

Three days before the show, Ms. Banta and I sit on her porch drinking chamomile tea. It's a little chilly, but warm for January, and the cool breeze feels nice on our faces. "Are you excited?" she asks.

I shrug. "I like when people laugh, but I'm also sooo nervous being up there."

"I bet it will all click at showtime." She takes a sip of her tea and pushes the blue cookie tin toward me. "They have some new varieties."

I pick through the fancy wrappers and choose a chocolate-covered graham cracker. "At least seeing you in the audience jumping and waving will make it easier."

Ms. Banta taps her cookie to her lips three times and takes a bite. Suddenly, she leaps up. "Did we take in all the bags? I want to make sure nothing else needs refrigerating."

Mama dropped me off half an hour ago, and Ms. Banta has checked each bag I brought from the store twice. "You got them all," I say.

"Be right back," she says, walking into the house. I see the light go on in the kitchen and imagine she's checking the temperature in the refrigerator again.

When she returns, I put down my cookie. Maybe she needs to rest. "I'll see you at the show, okay?"

Ms. Banta seems distracted. "The show. Right. It's highlighted in my planner." First the show, and then she'll be back at school. And Mrs. Nelson won't be able to do anything about it.

"You can sit in the front row with my mom and grandma," I say as I start walking down the steps.

"That would be lovely." She pastes a shaky smile on her face and burrows her hands in her sweater, pulling it around her.

When I get to the bottom of the steps, I turn around and look back at her porch, hoping she's jumping and waving like the last time I was here. Instead, I only see her back as she closes the screen door behind her.

Two days until the show, and the *whoosh* is constant.

Lacey bangs her legs against the seats as she watches the other acts. Since she already went, she's really impatient.

"Your dad couldn't even make it to one of the dress rehearsals?" she hisses as Val takes the stage.

It figures she'd start something when Val is no longer in the audience. She's braver when I don't have backup.

"I told you he has a gig. He'll be here for the show." I lace and unlace my fingers and rub my palms on my jeans.

"Good thing they already paid him. Otherwise who knows?"

"My dad would never bail," I snap.

Lacey just smiles, puts in her earbuds, and listens to her poetry music.

"Ready, Maya?" Ms. Franklin says.

Rattled, I walk slowly to the stage and climb up the steps.

"You can do it!" Val shouts, walking to a seat.

I try to shake off my nerves as I lift the mic from its stand. "Um, I-I only w-want to practice one joke."

"That's fine," Ms. Franklin says. "Today is about lighting, feeling comfortable onstage, sound check, all that. Don't worry."

I clear my throat. "Ain't it funny," I begin shakily, "how celebs are strange?" No, that's not it. That was so dumb. "Can I restart?" The light is shining in my face, and everyone is silent. I hear Barry cough. "Ain't it funny," I try again, "how, uh, celebrities collect things?" That's not that different from the original, but it throws me off. I'm so bad, even Barry's face is full of pity.

"It's okay, Maya," Ms. Franklin says. "It doesn't have to be perfect. We're really just making sure we can hear you. Why don't you work on stage presence?"

Stage presence. Got it. I practice taking the mic out of the stand and putting it back. Nice and easy. *Pretend like you're working the audience. Just like Dad.* But my hands are sweaty. I feel the mic slipping out of my hand, and I can't grab it. It hits the floor. *Clank!* The sound echoes loudly in the almost empty auditorium.

The faces blur together, but Lacey's smirk gets my attention. She makes sure our eyes lock before she gives me a thumbs-down. I can't take it. I run off the stage to the last row, positive Lacey's smirk is following me. My stomach clenches, and I feel puke rising up my throat. I swallow and try the backward alphabet. My eyes stare at the dirty floor. I count specks of garbage, too scared to look at anyone.

If Dad were here, he'd give me a pep talk. If Ms. Banta were here, she'd jump and cheer. *What if I quit right now? What would happen?* Nothing good, that's what. Mama and Baba need to see me perform comedy well if I want to bring our family back together. And what about Ms. Banta? Imagine her getting here—just for me—sitting in this crowd knowing how others feel about her, and then not even seeing me onstage? *Women in our family are strong. Letting thoughts control you is a weakness.* If I quit, that would be the end of my plan, and I'd never get the hot-hot-hot to stop.

I wince as I rub my hands together. They burn from all the washing I did this week and are covered in Band-Aids to protect the cracked skin that refuses to heal. "Gotta love winter, right?" Mama had said the other day, waving her hands in front of her face and showing me her own single (!) Band-Aid. "Just keep using the lotion I gave you." I need a new brain, not more lotion.

"Maya," Ms. Franklin says, concerned. She starts to get up, but I shake my head.

"I'm good. I just need some air," I say, rushing outside. The cold breeze snaps me out of my funk. *You got this.* My hands sting, but I ignore the burn. It's my punishment for even thinking about quitting. I've come too far to give up now.

CHAPTER 29

When I enter the store Friday after school, Mama's hair is frizzed and peeking out from her hairnet. Her lips are puckered, and her eyes are tired. She looks as stressed as I've been feeling—but unlike my worries, hers are not about the show. "Babushka and I will man the store, but we need your help with an order," she says.

"What kind of help?"

"Just some chicken cutlets and meatballs." Her voice is light, like she's suggested I only make a peanut butter and jelly sandwich. PB&J won't give someone salmonella. It won't be teeming with bacteria because the jelly wasn't spread on properly.

My cuts sting from beneath the Band-Aids.

You can do this. Breathe in, breathe out, I tell myself as I walk into the kitchen. I wash my hands again, replace the old Band-Aids with new ones, and put on a pair of gloves. Meatballs are quicker, so I tackle them first. *Crack.* Eggs go into the bowl, and I change gloves before adding breadcrumbs, seltzer, salt, and spices.

Deep breath. You're doing fine.

I return each item to the proper shelves before retrieving beef from the fridge. I've helped Babushka and Mama prepare cutlets and meatballs countless times, but today isn't a good day. I open the package of beef and spill the red juices into the trash before combining the meat with the ingredients in the bowl. My stained gloves mix bits of ground meat with the eggs—slimy yolks and whites coating the wormy-looking pieces. *Just keep kneading.* But this isn't the same as kneading dough. Dough stretches like mozzarella cheese. It doesn't drip like the raw pulp that's clinging to my latex-covered fingers. I form balls and arrange the rounded clumps in a pan, then shove the meatballs into the preheated oven.

Breathe in, breathe out.

New gloves replace the dirty, and my heart beats faster and faster as I get ready to make the cutlets. *It's just chicken. Get out the bowls, flour, eggs, and breadcrumbs.* I know it would have been easier to leave the ingredients out in the first place, but the thought of that chicken water splashing out of the bowl and contaminating everything around it is too much. Now I'm back to square one. An assembly line of bowls fills the counter—flour in one; breadcrumbs, eggs, and spices in others.

Red liquid trickles onto the floor as I tear open the package of chicken. My hands and fingers shake as they dip the pieces into the bowls. I check the gloves for rips, and even when I don't see any, I have to pause and take a breath. My brain fights with my eyes, trying to convince me there are slits I just don't see, that pieces of glove got into the cutlet, that pieces of chicken flesh seeped inside the gloves, under the Band-Aids, into the nicks on my skin.

"How's it going, Maya?" Mama calls into the kitchen, her head peeking in.

"Good, all good." Did I answer out loud or only in my head? I can't tell.

"Maya?" Suddenly, Mama is beside me, cool hand on my forehead. "Not warm," she mumbles, "but you don't look good."

"Am I done?" The words are a plea, not a question.

"Looks like. Let me just put the tray into the oven and set the timer."

When did I finish? I don't even remember placing the chicken pieces into the pan.

Beep. Beep. Beep. Each click of the timer is louder than the last.

"You forgot to set the timer for the meatballs, but they look like they need another ten minutes," she says after slicing one in half. She kisses me on the cheek and rests her hand on my forehead again. "If I'd known you were sick, I wouldn't have asked you to help." Her concern is about the store, not me.

"I'm just tired. The customers won't get sick." *They can't catch what I have.*

My apron is off, and the gloves are in the trash, but I don't remember removing either of them. I drag my feet into our bathroom and turn on the shower. Band-Aids fall off my hands as soap and hot water wash away any traces of meat and chicken flesh. I imagine everything pooling at my feet, washing into the drain. It's not until the water turns cold that I begin to breathe easier. The fog in my head thins enough to help me break through the steam, out of the bathroom, and into the cooler hallway air. All I have to do is get through the show. Once it's over, my family won't be broken anymore. And neither will I.

CHAPTER 30

"Come back here!" Julia shouts, chasing one of her juggling balls into the hallway.

"I forgot my headband," Reisha says, dumping everything from her tote onto the floor. "Now my hair will get in my eyes when I paint."

"Where's my chicken?" Derek moans.

It's thirty minutes to showtime, and backstage is in chaos. Val is huddled in a corner, her phone pressed against her ear, listening to the songs she'll be singing. Lacey smooths out her sheet of poems and sets it aside so she can finish putting on glittery makeup. She rummages in her bag, and Kat stands behind her, trying to brush her hair. I pace back and forth, trying all my strategies at once—from deep breaths to backward alphabet. *This is it. T-minus twenty minutes and counting. After today, hello, perfect Greenspan family, and goodbye, hot-hot-hot!* I peek into the auditorium, and my stomach flips when I see it's already more than half full and my dad still isn't here.

I text him. **Are you coming?**

Ten minutes away, he writes back. **NY traffic.**

I want to throw my phone. New York traffic is not new. He could have planned better. Especially when it's something important like this.

I text Ms. Banta. **Are you coming?**

Three dots appear, then disappear, then appear again.

"Maya," Ms. Franklin says, putting her hand on my arm. I shove the phone into my pocket. "You all right?"

"My dad still isn't here." I wipe my sweaty palms on my denim skirt.

She adjusts her gold headband. "We'll stall if we need to." She winks. "I know you've got this."

Ms. Franklin claps her hands for attention, and everyone freezes.

"Julia," she says, tossing her a tennis ball from the hallway, "this is yours. Reisha, lucky for you, I never leave home without scrunchies. Derek, I'm not sure about your chicken. Maybe ShopRite?"

Everyone laughs.

"It's an origami chicken," Derek says. "I'll raid the art room for paper."

"Sounds like we're all set," Ms. Franklin says.

Am I all set? Ms. Franklin wasn't worried about me, so I try to keep it that way.

"This was a mistake," Val moans. She checks her phone. "My grandparents aren't answering either."

I pull back the curtain again and spot Baba and Mama. They wave enthusiastically and blow me an air kiss. I do the same, while trying to hide my annoyance at Dad. Would it have killed him to follow regular people time this once? Just as tears threaten my eyes, he runs in the door. With ten minutes to spare—a record for him. I motion frantically for him to come backstage.

"You good?" he asks.

Help her, I mouth, grabbing his sleeve and dragging him to Val.

"Those sequins are star quality," he says.

Val takes a wet paper towel and dabs her face. "I thought I wanted the fame, Mr. Greenspan," she mutters, "but I was wrong."

I hide a smile at her theatrics. At least focusing on helping Val is stopping me from thinking about the hot-hot-hot and tingles.

Dad pulls up a chair beside her. "What you feel is normal. I'm always a wreck before shows."

Val puts down her paper towel. "Really?" she asks me.

I nod. "But once he takes the stage, you'd never know it."

"That's right," Dad chimes in. "I'm sure it will be the same for you."

"I was just hoping my grandparents—"

"They did," Dad says softly. "They were getting out of an Uber just as I was running in."

Val's eyes go wide, and it's like they're taking up her whole face. "For real?" She throws her arms around us, the color back in her face.

"My job here is done," Dad says. "Wish me luck."

I follow him out, the annoyance I felt earlier gone. He's here. That's what matters. "You're the best."

"Back at you, kid." He grins, but when he looks out at the full audience, he closes his eyes and takes a deep breath. He rubs his index finger across the bridge of his nose.

"Hey," he says, raising his fist to me.

I raise mine to his, and then we splay our fingers.

"*Kapow!*" we say together.

Val groans as applause, signaling the end of Lacey's performance, drifts into the dressing room.

I motion for her to join me behind the curtain as Dad begins his introduction. "Our next act," he booms, "will make you feel warm, despite her choice of songs. Please give a rousing welcome to Valerie Leone."

I put my arm around Val and gently push her forward. "You've got this."

Val nods and slowly walks to the mic. She gives a small wave to her grandparents and Joey as the sequins on her top sparkle under the lights. She takes a deep breath and grips the mic stand. The pianist gives her the intro to her first song, and she launches into her *Frozen* medley. She starts off low, voice a little shaky, but by the second bar, her voice soars through the audience. They shift in their seats, moving forward, hoping to get taken away on Val's musical magic carpet. She's comfortable now, moving across the stage, mic in hand. She easily picks up the piano cues and ends her four-song medley on a powerful crescendo.

"Let's hear it once more for Val!" Dad shouts. "She really *let that go*." Val takes a bow and blows kisses to the audience before running backstage.

"OH, EM, GEE!" She throws her arms around me. "That was amazing. I was nervous at first, but once the music picked up, something just came over me. I need to do that again. And again. I totally get your dad now. And guess what the best part was?"

My tingles have gotten worse, and I'm having trouble listening to her. "Best part?" I whisper, closing my eyes.

"Yes!" she seems to shout. "Joey was shouting and clapping, and my grandparents looked like they were going to cry . . ." Her voice trails off and when she speaks again, it sounds like she's going to cry, too. "They came in a car and are sitting in that stuffy, packed auditorium . . . for *me*!"

I'm really happy for her, but I'm feeling shaky. In minutes, I have to be on that stage, in front of all those people. I push my palms against my eyes.

Val squeezes herself into the tiny space beside me on my chair and gives me a hug. "Just focus on one person who's laughing, and you'll be fine. Better than fine—you'll be great!"

I nod just as I hear my dad introduce me.

"The next performer is a chip off the young block. Please welcome my daughter, Maya Greenspan."

As I walk onto the stage, I think about Dad's performance tricks. Even when he's nervous, he pretends he's not. I smile wide and imagine myself commanding the mic, tossing it from one hand to the other.

I give Dad a thumbs-up as he heads backstage, and quickly scan the crowd. No Ms. Banta. I close my eyes and think of the pages of jokes I've workshopped to get me here. I open my eyes and take a deep breath. Mama and Baba beam at me. I can do this.

"Ain't it funny," I begin, hands clutching the mic, "how parents are so proud of you until you do something dumb, and then it becomes 'Guess what *your* kid did today?' What if kids did that? Like my friend would say, 'Hey, is that your mom?' And I'd look at my mom's underwear static-clinging to the outside of her jeans and go, 'Nah, that's my *grandma's daughter*.'"

Some people laugh. It's a start. At least there wasn't dead silence. I look at the first row where Babushka and Mama are sitting, and they're both laughing. I glance at Dad, who's behind the curtain, and he winks at me. I follow with jokes about the Russian store.

"So, you all probably know my family owns The Russian Gourmet," I say. Some whoops and hollers from the audience. "If you like our place, then this joke is sooo not about you." More laughter. "Do you know the biggest question we get? 'What's fresh?' Let me tell you all something. *Everything* is fresh." Pause. "Even when it isn't." The crowd chuckles, and I see Babushka's jaw drop. "Kidding, kidding. My grandma looks like she's having one of those 'that's-somebody-else's-grandkid' moments."

I tell more jokes about the store, including one about people leaving their fingerprints all over the glass cases. "There's a sign," I begin, twirling the mic cord around my fingers, "that specifically says 'Do Not Touch Glass.' Of course, it's not a crime to do that, but if it were—or say we needed someone to help with cleaning those cases—we'd catch the culprit every time—we've already got your fingerprints!"

The crowd laughs again, and I finally get it. The laughter is like a trampoline pushing me forward. The crowd isn't making me nervous anymore. I already made them laugh. I can do it again! But I wish Ms. Banta were here, jumping up and down like she promised. I'm working on conquering my fear, but what about hers?

Speaking of fears . . . I launch into my final joke about the kid who hoards my pencils. Of course, I don't say Barry's name, and I try to leave out details that would make him look bad. "Ain't it funny," I begin as I walk across the stage, "how some kids have blankies they latch onto? Well, I have pencils. They come in so many colors, and when you put them by your cheek like this . . ." My voice gets dreamy as I pretend to snuggle next to an imaginary pencil. People giggle. "Well, this boy in my class asked why I have so many pencils. It's obvious. What if something happens to one, or two." I pause. "Or six." The audience laughs again. "What? Those pencil sharpeners are hungry, and I'm too old to bring a blankie to school!

"And that's my time," I say as I put the mic back in its holder. "Thanks, everyone. I hope tonight my dad will say, 'That's my kid!'" People whistle and applaud. I hear Dad's thunderous clap as he jogs onstage. "My kid, y'all!" he says, giving me a huge bear hug. I blush and take a bow but not before seeing the tears in his eyes. *We did this*, I think. Just like "we" did that killer set that got him Artie.

I'm not even fully backstage when Val pounces on me and almost knocks me over. "You killed it! Holy moly! Your dad better watch out."

"You really thought I was good?" I flop down on a chair. It's over now, but then why is my stomach all jumpy and why are my hands clammy?

Val searches my face. "You couldn't tell based on all the laughter? You were awesome! You walked and talked and paused in the right places. You did EVERYTHING! I'm so glad we have different talents, or I'd be totally jelly." She hugs me again.

She's right. I did it *all*. And I *loved* it. It was just like my dad said. You're nervous before, but once you get onstage, it's just you and the audience. What's more, I'm so proud of myself. Which is why it makes no sense that my head is full of cotton. "Water?" I croak.

In seconds, an open water bottle is thrust into my hands. "Drink," Val says, voice panicked.

I do, and the spots lessen. "Maybe I'm getting sick or something."

She gives me two packets of saltine crackers and stares at me until I finish all of them. The spots are gone, but my stomach still feels a little queasy. I drink more water and flash my brightest smile at Val. "That helped a lot. It's probably because I was too nervous to eat much today."

She studies me, then pulls over a chair so she can watch the rest of the show from behind the curtain. She motions for me to do the same with my chair. Each time I feel Val's eyes on me, I pull the sides of my mouth into a smile. I try to be Maya the Comedian, not Maya, Queen Worrier. My hands get clammier and clammier, and the pebble in my stomach grows bigger and bigger. Soon, I can barely hear the performers over the *whoosh* in my head.

"How great was our girl?" Mama says when the four of us get home that night.

"Stupendous!" Dad says, raising his glass of sparkling apple juice.

Mama, Baba, and I raise our glasses, too. I feel better seeing all of us together. Maybe it was just the heat of the lights and the excitement that triggered the *whoosh*. I barely hear it now.

"I could have done without the store jokes," Baba says, "but you were wonderful."

"I think I felt it," I tell them, "that *pop, pop, pop* Dad feels when he's onstage."

"Oh boy," Dad says, "we're in trouble now." His eyes sparkle, and I feel closer to him than ever.

"Seeing you up there made me remember your dad's early stand-up days," Mama says.

"Those were good times," Dad says, putting his hand on Mama's arm. Unlike the rehearsal where Dad hugged her, she doesn't move away.

This is perfect. It's all happening. My phone pings, but it's only Val, which reminds me it's not *all* happening. "Did Ms. Banta call you to say she couldn't make it?"

"I'm sorry, Maya," Mama says, "but she didn't."

"Not everyone is as strong as you, Maya," Baba says. "She just couldn't power through."

"Mama," my mother says sharply to Baba. *"Chvatzit."* Enough.

I jiggle my foot under the table. I'm glad they don't know that I had trouble powering through after the show.

"What are the weekend plans?" Mama asks Dad.

As Dad tells Mama about a new restaurant he wants to take me to, I wonder how long before he can move back home. Then, we can finally tell Mama about the spots I've seen.

I hug Mama and Baba goodbye, and they don't look sad like the first time I went with Dad. That's definitely a good sign, too.

"Thanks for all your help," I say when Dad and I get on the highway.

"Anytime, sweetheart. You and I are a good team."

"Even Baba thought it was good."

Dad laughs. "That's the highest praise."

I look out the window at the New York City skyline as we speed down the highway. "I was thinking—if your travel gigs are during my school breaks, Mama and I can go with you." Something shifts in Dad's face, but I barrel on. "Oh, right. You'll probably perform in eighteen-and-over places. Well, just you and Mama can go then."

Dad's eyebrows furrow and his mouth twitches. "Your mom can't just up and leave the store."

"Baba and I can run it. It wouldn't be every weekend." Doesn't he understand they have to do things together? Be part of each other's worlds again? "You would have to help more at the store, though. So you both can reach your dreams, you know?" And so I can be cool-cool-cool.

Dad taps his fingers on the steering wheel and checks his rearview mirror. He puts on his blinker and eases into the Lincoln Tunnel. We are met with bumper-to-bumper traffic, but we have nowhere to be. "Maya, we *are* both following our dreams," he says softly.

What is he not understanding? Didn't he see that Mama didn't move away when he put his hand on her arm? They get along so well. And after my set, I know she finally realizes how important comedy is to us. "Yeah, I know, but like together. When are you moving back home?"

He wraps his hands around the steering wheel until his knuckles turn white. "I *have* a home. In New York."

"Well, yeah, for now. I know you have a lease—" I ramble.

His face looks so pained that I know he does understand. But it doesn't make sense.

"You and Mama said the hours didn't work. You said you couldn't be there for us like you wanted. But now you have a chance. You get how hard it is to run the store, and you've been helping. She understands the comedy thing, and you have Artie now, so you don't need all those midnight gigs. Wasn't the plan to move back home once all this stuff was figured out?"

He pulls me to him. "That wasn't the plan. Too much has changed between us over time."

I pull away from him. "Did Mama know you never planned on coming back? Does *she* know that wasn't the plan?"

"We decided together. Even with a manager, my life doesn't change that much. There will be more opportunities, but I'll still have to be ready for last-minute gigs. It's not fair to you or your mom if I drop things last minute—and that's what I'll have to do. We both have to give our all to our own dreams and figure out who we are apart from each other."

"But I got onstage." I say it like it's everything.

"And I'm so proud of you for that. Mama is, too." The cars start to move a little, and Dad inches up in the tunnel.

My eyes fill with tears, and I try to hold them back.

"I'm so sorry, Maya," Dad says. "I thought you knew this move was permanent."

"How could I have known?" I shout. "You're not even divorced!"

"That takes time," he says weakly. "The law requires a separation before we get divorced." The cars are fully moving now, and we keep pace with them.

I'm sure that law exists so people can change their minds. Like I thought they were going to.

"And you're still wearing—" I start, but he suddenly brakes hard, and his hands shift on the steering wheel. His bare finger mocks me.

He's *not* still wearing his ring. How's that for a callback?

I let my tears flow, and I'm glad Baba can't see me. They spill down my cheeks, but for what? No matter how many more fall, they won't change anything.

CHAPTER 31

"Since you all worked so well together at the show," Ms. Franklin says Monday morning, "I made a partner list for today's math work."

Somehow, I just know what's in store for me. I put my head on my desk, hoping to block out the inevitable, but in seconds Barry's chair is beside mine.

"Let's go," he says. "I hate finishing last."

The familiar hot-hot-hot starts, and I hate it more than ever. It wasn't supposed to be here today. My plan was supposed to work, and the hot and tingles were going to be bad memories. Poof! Gone. I got through the talent show, but that was because getting through it meant good things were coming. Now there's nothing at the end of the dark tunnel.

"How do you want to do this?" I ask, slowly opening my workbook. "I don't think we have to do *every* problem together." *Or any.*

"How about we check in after every five problems?" he asks. He puts his saliva-covered pencil on his desk, and I can't focus on the problems because I'm afraid the spit is going to ooze to my side. "Hello? After five, okay?"

"Fine," I squeak.

He taps his pencil, and a little spittle sprays onto the tip of my desk. *Deep breaths, deep breaths.* I get paper towels and cover the parts of my desk closest to his.

"What's wrong with you? You were so different onstage," he grumbles. "I actually thought this would be fun."

He thought working with me would be fun? He makes my life miserable every day! "Let's just do the problems," I mumble.

My hands shake as I move the ruler to measure the objects in my book. He finishes his problems quickly and sighs loudly. The longer I take, the more Barry bounces in his seat and bites on his pencil.

"Finally!" he almost shouts when I finish the last problem. "Do you want to just read off your answers, or will that take forever, too?"

My clothes are sticking to me, and there's a rushing sound in my ears. I want to move the paper towels and go faster, but I can't. I speedily recite my answers so we can move on.

Each time Barry measures, the ruler scrapes loudly across his desk. "Shoot!" he says suddenly. He sheepishly holds up a broken pencil. "Can I borrow one of yours? Please? It really was an accident." I believe that he didn't break the point on purpose, but my hands shake anyway.

I toss a red pencil onto his desk and do a mental inventory of the colors I have left. Orange, green, blue, indigo, violet.

He says something about me being grouchy, but between the *whoosh* and desperately trying to focus on the last two problems, I can barely hear him.

"Done," I whisper.

Barry frowns. "Seriously, it's just math. Chill."

I put my hand in my pocket to squeeze Pinkie.

He stares at me. "Why can't you just act normal?"

I wish I knew the answer.

CHAPTER 32

"Maya, are you listening?" Mama says on Wednesday at The Russian Gourmet. "I said Ms. Banta called twice."

I busy myself with arranging my hairnet and putting on my gloves, so I can ignore Mama a little longer.

"Maya."

"What do you want me to say? We had a plan. I kept up my end, but she bailed." I glance at the entrance. The line is getting longer by the second. It's just a matter of time before I can exit this conversation. To be honest, I don't even know if I'm mad at Ms. Banta anymore or even at my parents. I'm just sad and lost and out of ideas for how to fix my brain.

Mama's expression softens. "Not everything is black and white, *Zaichik*."

She said the same to me last weekend when I came home from Dad's. It all looked zebra to me, though.

Ding! Babushka rings the bell to let us know she needs us. Now.

Mrs. Nelson is waiting, but at least her nonsense is expected. "How can I help you?"

"What's fr—?" she begins, then catches herself. "Never mind. It's all fresh, even when it isn't, right?"

"It was just a joke," I stammer.

"I know," she snaps. "I *do* have a sense of humor."

"I'm sorry," I say sincerely. "I'm happy to help."

"Just pack whatever as long as it will feed four," she says in her usual snippy tone. It makes me feel more jittery than usual.

"Appetizers, dinner, and dessert?"

She moves closer to the counter and is about to lean on it, then steps back. No doubt because of my fingerprints joke. Her face looks both annoyed and flustered. "Sure. Sounds good. Don't let anyone say *I* don't know how to be nice or compromise."

Mrs. Nelson paces in front of the register while I count out four chicken kabobs and enough rice, grilled veggies, salad, and cake to feed her family. As I pack, she keeps giving me pointed looks that imply I'm not moving fast enough. Barry has been my partner for the last two days, and I've gotten enough looks and comments about how slow I am to last a lifetime. I don't need the same from Mrs. Nelson.

She puffs out her chest and leans in close. "I wasn't going to come here anymore," she says in Russian.

My hands itch inside my gloves. "Why's that?"

Babushka overhears and takes over, bringing all of her food to the register. "What's this about, Karina?" she asks.

I stop what I'm doing so I can listen.

Mrs. Nelson waves her hands toward the cameras. "Everyone is willing to just sweep it all under the rug and not protect our children."

"I don't need protecting," I say, and Mama glares at me and shakes her head.

Mrs. Nelson laughs. "I'd beg to differ. You're always so jumpy. Your hands were even shaking while packing my food."

I grit my teeth as her voice cuts through me. Can everyone tell something's wrong with me? Can they always tell?

Babushka quickly rings up her food and shoves it into a bag. "That will be sixty dollars."

Mrs. Nelson takes a crumpled paper out of her pocket. Names cover the front and back. "See this? All the people in town who feel like I do. And you know what I was told? That it's discrimination to fire someone for mental health! Like I'm a villain for wanting to take care of our kids."

"Sixty dollars," Babushka says again.

Mrs. Nelson throws three twenties beside the cash register and storms out.

I run to the bathroom and take a deep breath in as soap covers my stiff, peeling hands. Slowly, I stretch new gloves over my cuts. The latex feels especially sticky today.

I look in the mirror and try to see myself as Mrs. Nelson does. How long before she starts a petition against me?

Clank. Clank. Clank.

I bolt up in bed and look at my clock. 11:30. Has this noise replaced the *whoosh*? *Clank.* No, this is definitely coming from downstairs, not my brain. I creep to the staircase, see the light in the kitchen, and take comfort in the fact that it's just Babushka and Mama cleaning up. But their raised voices stop me from going back to bed.

"She hasn't been the same since the show," Babushka says.

"Please, Mama." *Clank.*

"This is his fault," Baba says. "Who knows if he'll be around now that his *dream* is coming true?"

Mama slams something onto the counter. "Just stop. Not everything is about him."

"You're right about that," Baba says, scraping something. "The *two* of you are to blame. That poor girl. You and James acting like you do. I told you having him here for Chanukah was a bad idea. Why *wouldn't* she think you were getting back together?"

"Some things are gray, Mama."

Baba snorts.

"Besides," Mama continues, talking over Baba's mutterings, "I've been thinking about something. What if what Maya told us is true?"

A clang of dishes. "What are you talking about?"

"Those pages she showed us," Mama says. "I've been reading more—"

The faucet turns on. "Now *you're* believing that *choosh*?"

"But what Karina said wasn't all wrong," Mama says. "Hasn't Maya been looking more scared lately? You should have seen her face when she was making chicken."

A chair scrapes across the floor. "So, what are you saying, Sarah? She has that *psihoz*, like her teacher?"

I don't wait to hear Mama's answer. Things *have* been getting worse since the show—since *before* the show, even, but I don't know why. My plan crashing and burning hasn't helped either. Mama and Dad had their dreams, but getting them back together and stopping the hot-hot-hot was mine.

Maybe I do have this *psihoz*. *Psihoz* is more than anxiety. It means crazy. Like how the petition people see Ms. Banta. After all, what normal person would be so laser focused on their plan succeeding that they'd miss all the signs telling them it didn't stand a chance?

Breathe through your nose for four.

Clank goes a plate in the kitchen.

Hold for a count of seven.

Clank. Clank.

Slowly breathe out through your mouth for a count of eight.

Clank. Whoosh.

When I was little, Mama tucked me in "like a hot dog in a bun." I try to do the same now, making myself small and folding the blankets tightly around my arms and legs.

Downstairs, the clanking gets louder and the voices more irritated, but I burrow deeper and deeper beneath the blanket, making it harder and harder to hear them.

CHAPTER 33

"Working with Barry all week must have been torture," Val says at our lockers on Friday.

This whole week has been terrible. The *whoosh* and hot-hot-hot have not let up, and this morning has been the worst. I press my palms against my eyes until multicolored spots swim behind my eyelids.

"Maya? Maya?"

"Mmm?" I push my fingers into the ridges of our lockers to take the focus away from the noise.

"Come in! Come in!" Ms. Franklin singsongs, her voice somehow flying above the *whoosh*.

Feet stomp around me, and colors merge together.

"Come on!" Val calls, grabbing my hand and dragging me into the classroom. My legs wobble as I walk to my desk.

"Let's go," Barry hisses, but I don't know where he wants me to go. Ms. Franklin must have given a direction, but her voice is too quiet now. "Maya!"

I press my hands against my ears and put my head on my desk. I need to get out of here.

Someone grips my arm. "Ms. Franklin," Val says. Her voice sounds so far away. "Maya needs to go to the nurse."

Val's arm squeezes mine as she tries to pull me up. Her breath tickles my ear. "Let's go."

I let her guide me to the door.

"Don't hurl!" Derek shouts.

The class laughs, but I don't care. I'd rather they think I'm going to throw up than decide I have some kind of *psihoz*.

Val slams the door shut, and I sink to the floor beside the lockers.

"Are you going to be sick?" she asks, voice shaking.

"No," I whisper.

"But something's wrong, isn't it?" I should be able to tell Val, but I can't. There are too many words. Too many things to explain.

"Is it like with the elastics?" she asks. "The hot-hot-hot?"

I think I nod.

"What happened?" Ms. Graham asks, suddenly beside us. Did Ms. Franklin call her?

"Working with Barry all week made her sick," Val says. "He'll do that to anyone."

She forces a laugh, but I can tell she's just pretending. I hear the worry in her voice. I remember seeing Ms. Banta on the floor of our store, lost and panicked. Do I look that way to Val?

"Thank you, Val, I'll take it from here."

Val squeezes my shoulder, and I hear the door close behind her as she walks back into the classroom.

In her office, Ms. Graham gently unclenches my fingers and wraps them around a paper cup of water. "Drink, please." I do, and she refills the cup and instructs me to drink again.

"Was Val scared?" I whisper, a lump forming in my throat.

"She'll be fine," Ms. Graham says. "Focus on the water in your mouth. Swish it around before swallowing."

I do as she says, trying to force the cold liquid past the rock in my throat. *Just think cold, cold, cold.* Water brushes the inside of my cheeks and rests on my tongue. I swallow and imagine it pushing the rock down into my belly.

"Good," Ms. Graham coaxes. "Do it again."

The *whoosh* is a dull roar, and Ms. Graham's voice sounds closer. I swallow again. This time, I feel the cold more.

"Can you look at me, Maya?"

I take a deep breath and slowly open my eyes. Spots form at the edges of the room, but Ms. Graham's face isn't blurry.

"Let's try something, okay?" she says.

My heart beats quickly. The *whoosh* threatens to swallow me at any second.

"Look around the room and tell me five things you see," Ms. Graham says, eyes not leaving my face.

"You, the glass container filled with cotton balls." It takes a lot of energy to force the words out. "The peeling paint on the walls, the cracked gray tile, the papers on your desk." I scoot to the back of the cot so I can rest my back against the wall.

"That was very good." Her voice is encouraging and soothing. "Now name four things you can touch."

"The plaster behind me." I move my fingers to the flowers on my jeans. "The raised puffy paint." My hand slides across the pleather cot. "The soft foam."

"Just one more!" I can't help but smile at Ms. Graham's enthusiasm. Ain't it funny but also sad that such minor things seem so big to her? Ain't it funny but also sad that these tiny tasks seem so big to me, too?

I feel around for a fourth thing. "The cold metal of the cot."

"Terrific! Now, tell me three things you hear."

I close my eyes. "The kids laughing as they're waiting to get into the gym, someone running down the hallway, the crackling of the intercom." It's not until I finish listing that I realize I don't hear the *whoosh* anymore.

"Two more senses. Are you feeling all right to continue?"

"Definitely."

"Tell me two things you smell."

I inhale. "The yucky antiseptic smell. Ummm . . ."

Ms. Graham places something wrapped in my hand. "Smell."

I bring the wrapper to my nose. "Chocolate!"

Ms. Graham laughs. "Good job. And this will bring us to our last one."

I open my eyes. "May I use some sanitizer, please?" I ask, knowing what's coming next. There is no way I'm touching that piece of chocolate after my fingers have felt so many germy things.

I place the wrapped candy in my lap while Ms. Graham squirts sanitizer on my palms.

"Ready?" she asks after I've rubbed my hands together carefully to not aggravate the cuts. "Name one thing you taste."

I unwrap the mini Milky Way and pop it into my mouth. "There's chocolate," I say, mouth full. "And caramel." The pieces stick to my teeth, and it's the best Milky Way I've ever tasted.

"This is something you can also do on your own when things get overwhelming." Ms. Graham pauses. "Now, let's talk a little about what happened today."

"Something like this happened before," I say quietly, remembering when I made the cutlets and meatballs.

"But this was worse, right?"

I nod. "It's never been this bad."

"It's called a panic attack," Ms. Graham says. "It's important for you to have support to work through these feelings."

The *whoosh* is starting again, and clamminess sets in. Support means family. "I already tried telling my mom, grandma, and dad. They don't understand."

Ms. Graham nods. "I'll help them understand."

Baba's word pricks at my ribs again. "They'll think there's something wrong with me."

Ms. Graham takes a deep breath. "There's nothing wrong with you, Maya. People just don't know how to react to something unfamiliar."

I lace my fingers together. "But what if I *do* have what Ms. Banta has? She didn't even come to my show."

Ms. Graham reaches over and takes my hand. "She feels really bad about that. The two of you should talk sometime. But I want you to understand something. Anxiety is not the same for everyone. One bad day, even a few weeks of bad days, doesn't define who you are."

I tap my fingers on the cot while she searches the computer for my parents' numbers. "So, you don't think I'm crazy?" I blurt.

She steps away from the computer and sits beside me. "I really don't like that word, so let's not use it. Especially to describe yourself. Everyone has something they're battling. Anxiety just happens to be your fight."

"I don't want Val to think there's something wrong with me," I whisper.

Ms. Graham pats my hand. "I'm sure she doesn't see it that way."

What I *don't* say is that I have other fears. Like that Babushka and Mama will see things differently from Ms. Graham. Or, even worse, Baba will keep blaming Dad for causing this.

CHAPTER 34

Ms. Graham asks me to wait outside her office while she talks to Mama. I try to listen through the door, but I only hear murmuring.

"Come on, *Zaichik*," Mama says when she finally walks into the hallway. She holds my hand like when I was little, and we walk to the car. I don't care if someone sees. Her fingers wrapped around mine make me feel safe.

"Today must have been scary," she says when we're inside the car.

"It still is."

Mama strokes my hair and turns on the music. "Baba is preparing dough so you can bake cookies together."

I show her my cracked skin. "No."

"The cold weather," she begins, but stops when I turn away from her.

"I'm sorry. I don't know what to say."

"Can we just go home?" I ask. "And can you tell Baba I don't want to talk?"

Mama nods and steps out of the car to call Baba. She looks annoyed when she gets back a few minutes later. "I see it went well," I say.

"Ha." She pulls out of the parking lot. "Your grandma loves you, Maya. You know that, right? She's just worried about you."

Because she thinks there's something wrong with me. "I know."

"Also, I called your dad when Ms. Graham called me, and he really wants to see you tonight. He's almost here."

I rest my head on the window.

Mama squeezes my knee. "Everything will be okay."

I nod, and we drive home in silence.

Dad and I sit on the bleachers of the High Line, staring out at the city below us. The colors from the traffic lights blend with those of the brakes and headlights, racing past my eyes, faster and faster. Dad alternates between sitting beside me and walking to the barrier. Back and forth, back and forth—the Worry Waltz.

"I'm sorry 'the Maya problem,'" I form air quotes with my fingers, "is ruining your happy place."

He lets out a large exhale, the smoke from his breath billowing into the sky, and sits beside me. "You're not a problem. I blame myself."

I trace circles on the metal bench with my index finger. "Why do parents always say stuff like that? It just makes me feel worse."

He grimaces. "Now *I* feel worse for making *you* feel worse."

"Ha ha." I lightly punch his arm and snuggle into his bomber jacket. "I'm surprised we're here instead of having a big discussion at the kitchen table."

Dad blows on his hands and rubs them together. "Yeah... your mom and I thought it would be better if you hung out with me tonight. No spots, though."

"You told her?"

Dad runs his hand through his hair. "Breaking that promise to her was a big mistake on my part."

"But—"

"No, baby. I should never have encouraged that. We kept a secret when she assumed I was keeping my promise. That was wrong."

I bite my lip. "Was Mama mad?"

He shrugs. "She was annoyed, but we're just concerned about making sure you're okay right now." He kisses my head.

I tap my sneakers on the ground and rub my hands on my jeans. I've been wanting to talk with him about this for so long, but now that I have the chance, it's all too much.

"I should have said something sooner," he says. "I noticed signs, like some of the food things and how you'd get jittery, but I was hoping I was wrong. That it was just regular kid stuff."

Whoosh. All I hear is that he noticed signs, that I always look jumpy—just like Mrs. Nelson said. "You were hoping your daughter was normal?" My voice is so tiny, I don't know if he hears it.

He takes my hands in his and squeezes. "No! Nothing like that. It's because of me."

I face him. "What do you mean?"

"I know what it's like," he says, "to have so many thoughts in your head, to go back and forth between highs and lows, to feel so trapped by nervousness you just want to sleep because then you don't have to think. I didn't want that for you."

I think about how he sometimes seems lost and how he looked frantic because we had forgotten to do the *kapow*. Funny how I also saw signs but didn't put any of them together.

A tear falls down my cheek. "It stinks, doesn't it?"

He pulls me to him and wraps his arms around me. "It does."

He definitely understands now, so I want to explain more. "My stuff is not exactly like yours."

"Tell me then."

I take a deep breath. "I have all the things you have. But I also get this . . . I call it the hot-hot-hot. It's, like, the feeling you get before taking a test, and it just spreads."

He nods and rubs his goatee. "I've had that. And your head feels like it's kind of underwater?"

"Yes!" I pause. "I wanted to tell you sooner, but then you said everyone worries, so . . ." My voice trails off.

"Oh, Maya. I'm so sorry. I thought I was making it better. Feeling like this can be scary. I'm an adult and it's scary for *me*, so I was trying to spare you." He hugs me tighter. "You said you felt other things, too?"

"Yeah, so besides the hot thing, I need patterns? Like if Barry takes a pencil and messes up my pattern, it *causes* the hot, and makes me feel off all day. Then, I get a thought in my head, and it doesn't go away."

"That sounds really hard." He kisses the top of my head. "I'm always here for you, and I will always listen now. Okay?"

I nod and face him. Tears run down my cheeks, but this time I do feel better.

I close my eyes and try to focus on the honking and street noise. The *whoosh* quiets. I want him to be okay, too. "When you're onstage, you're happy, right?"

He nods. "It's just me, the audience, the heat of the lights. And I'm sailing high for hours after until—"

"You're not." I think about how Dad acts before his shows, and before that when he's trying to come up with material, how anxious he seems, how twitchy his mouth and eyes get sometimes.

"Right," he says. "It's a hard way to live. But," he smiles wide, "the fact that we're catching this early with you is awesome."

I snort. "Yeah, *so* awesome."

He shakes his head. "No, it really is. In time, there will be far fewer episodes like this."

"Maybe," I say, "but Baba and Mama think I'm broken."

The creases on Dad's forehead knit together. "I think you misunderstood."

I shake my head. "I heard them talking. Baba used the word *psihoz*."

Dad flinches. "I hate that word."

"But she could be right."

Dad puts his arm around me. "Your grandma is scared. Your mom is, too."

"So, you don't think people will say things about me? Remember all the comments everyone posted on that video of Ms. Banta?" I shiver.

Dad lifts my chin. "Maya, I'd be lying if I said you won't meet more people like Mrs. Nelson and Mrs. Antonov. But you didn't scare off Val. She's texted you ten times already to check in. I think there will be more Vals than the others. And we'll give you tools my family didn't believe in when I was growing up—tools it seems like Ms. Banta didn't have either."

"And Baba?"

Dad sighs. "Baba is a hard sell. It's not all her fault. The way she grew up, having to hide her feelings so her mother wouldn't worry . . . We'll work on her."

The *we'll* makes me wince. "The reason I was really upset you wouldn't be at rehearsals was that I thought it would bring you and Mama together. I had this whole plan."

Heat rushes to my cheeks, and for a second I feel dumb for thinking the plan could work. But then I think about being onstage, doing something I *never* thought I could—and being good at it.

That thought should make me happy, but the outcome still hurts. My voice breaks. "I guess trying to get you and Mama back together was stupid."

"No, sweetie. That wasn't stupid at all. I miss you both so much, but my life isn't changing. I'll be traveling more. If a great gig comes up, I'll still need to take it. And all this," he waves his arm around his body, "still needs a lot of work. When I'm down, I drag everyone down with me."

I pull away from him. "That's not true at all! You never drag me down." Except that's not totally true. That night he was stressed because of Highlights, I fed on that and got all nervous, too. When he was sad about his career, I just wanted to help him feel better. And his lateness to the talent show made the tingles worse, too.

"Your mom has done a great job covering for me, but that isn't fair to her. Sometimes, my sadness covers the whole house. And not all of it can be turned into comedy, no matter how much time passes."

We stare at the speeding cars, the racing lights, the people below us. Everyone rushing, running, and getting mashed into one big ball of color. I imagine all our worries crashing to the ground, mixing with the colors, being left forever in the chaos below. And I think about dreams and how Mama and Dad are following theirs. Maybe I need a dream that's just about me, too. One that I can control.

CHAPTER 35

A week later, Mama, Dad, and I sit together in a clean, warm therapist's office. We met with Dr. Tracey a few days ago to discuss what I've been experiencing, and now we're back to talk about next steps.

"Maya," Dr. Tracey says as I play with the fringe on a blue throw pillow, "when we met, you mentioned the tingles, the *whoosh*, and your heart thumping a lot." I feel like the ground is slowing moving away from my toes. She leans forward in her chair, tucks a piece of dark hair behind her ear, and tugs her black leather skirt past her knees. These little movements show me she worries about stuff, too, and make me feel better. "I want you to know," she continues, "that all these things are normal. And I will help you get them under control."

"Isn't that great news, honey?" Mama says, her voice too optimistic.

Dr. Tracey's smile wavers. "It *is* great news, but it's not a quick fix. When someone has generalized anxiety disorder, the scary feelings often jump from one event to the next, so even if a stressful situation is over, the emotion latches on to something else. Maya also has OCD tendencies, which affect the anxiety and vice versa." Mama's face clouds, but the words help me understand what happened after the talent show.

One scary event was done, but the anxiety just lay in wait until it could find a new host. Then, when other things worried me—like bringing my parents together and Barry—it just kept jumping from one thing to the next, gaining power, triggering the OCD.

I think about my patterns with the pencils and Ms. Banta's patterns. Are we the same?

Could my anxiety build up like Ms. Banta's and explode?

"There's something else that worries me," I tell Dr. Tracey, while I look at my feet.

I tell her about Ms. Banta's patterns, and how I thought she was getting better because there were fewer of them, but then she had the breakdown in the store. The *whoosh* gets louder. "Do you think she has OCD, too? Like me?" I squeak out.

Dr. Tracey shakes her head. "I haven't met her," she says gently, "so I do not feel comfortable diagnosing her. Let's focus on you. You exhibit GAD and some OCD, but it all falls on a spectrum. No one person presents exactly the same as someone else. However, even though it appears on the outside like someone with GAD or OCD is doing better, that's not always the case. And sometimes, when things are actually getting worse, to avoid standing out to others, people may try to hide their behaviors. But that can make the situation more difficult."

That makes sense. When I try to stop my urge to handwash, the thought just keeps coming back, and my hands tingle, and the more I try *not* to think about it, the worse it gets. Maybe the same thing was happening with Ms. Banta when she broke her own patterns.

"And think about when you had your panic attack; it took time and a lot of things building up to have a big reaction like that. I could see something similar having been the case for Ms. Banta as well. Again," Dr. Tracey cautions, "those are my thoughts without meeting her. I'm sure some of that would change if I talked to her directly. But the kind of reaction she had in your store isn't the norm, and now that we're working together, we'll be able to talk through everything together to help you control things before they get to an explosion point."

It helps to have all this explained in pieces.

"What can *we* expect?" Mama asks.

"Well," Dr. Tracey says, "each week, I will give Maya an exercise to practice."

"Even if I'm feeling fine . . . ?" I begin, my voice trailing off.

Dr. Tracey cocks her head, like Ms. Banta and Ms. Franklin do when they listen. "Especially then. If you master some techniques when you're calm, then it's easier to pull them out when you need them the most." She smiles at me. "Maya, I'd like to talk a little about one thing you mentioned at our first meeting."

I mentioned many things. "Which one?"

"You believing that controlling what's around you can stop your anxiety."

My face burns. I don't want her to discuss my plan now. I look down at my feet.

But Dr. Tracey seems to understand, because she says, "For example, always stressing about that boy taking your pencils. That's not something you can control. I don't want you thinking, *If only a, b, c happened, the anxiety would disappear.* That just sets you up for disappointment since the world isn't perfect."

I look up at her and smile. I know all about disappointment.

"So," she continues to Mama and Dad, "I want Maya to have the tools to handle her own emotions and thoughts regardless of what is happening around her." She turns to me. "You're a brave girl. You've been through a lot. You got up onstage! I could never do that. And here you are. The more you feel confident being in charge of the hot-hot-hot, the less buildup of these feelings you'll have."

I don't agree with everything she said, especially the brave part, but I nod. I like the part about me owning my feelings rather than them owning me.

Dr. Tracey looks at her notepad. "I would like us all to try an exercise today."

Mama shifts nervously in her seat, but Dad leans forward, elbows on his knees, raring to go.

"Let's begin," says Dr. Tracey, "by picturing things that bother you."

I close my eyes and picture Barry's fingers on my pencils, Mrs. Nelson's petition, and Lacey's smug face.

"Everyone have something?" Dr. Tracey asks.

"Yes," we all say.

"Great," Dr. Tracey continues. "Now, imagine that all these worries are in one room beside an open window."

"Check," Dad says.

"You want to get these images to the other side of the window, out of the room. Imagine pushing the worries away and the window shutting."

I remember trying to calm my thoughts before when I was at my dad's. I had no success then. Now, it takes effort, but I get them to the other side.

"How was that?" Dr. Tracey asks.

"They quieted down," Dad says. "Eventually."

Dr. Tracey nods. "The key is to keep trying and not feel defeated. It's a process."

Mama clears her throat. "How long of a process?"

Dr. Tracey's smile quivers. "Elaborate, please?"

Mama wrings her hands. "Well, I mean," she stammers, "if we help Maya, and she does all the exercises, how long before the anxiety is completely gone?" Her voice falters as Dad puts his hand on her arm.

"It doesn't really work like that," he says softly. Then he looks at Dr. Tracey. "Right?"

Dr. Tracey nods. "Right," she says gently. "Anxiety and OCD don't just disappear."

Tingles push at the tips of my toes. "Ever?" I ask.

Dr. Tracey gives me a sympathetic smile and shakes her head. "I'm afraid not, but it's not all bad."

I give her a questioning look as the tingles rise to my ankles.

"Take the OCD, for instance," Dr. Tracey says. "To the extreme, it's not helpful. However, small amounts of it—like if you want to get your report just right or," she turns to my dad, "spend hours working on that one punch line—help us accomplish our goals." She pauses and looks at Mama. "Our goal is to help Maya be in control."

"So," I say slowly, "I'll be able to eventually control the hot-hot-hot, and it won't always be so . . ." I search for the right word. "Big?"

"That's right!" Dr. Tracey says. "We *all* worry, but we want you to be the boss. If it feels like too much, I want you to have tools to bring it down. Does that make sense?"

I'd be able to push the hot-hot-hot and *whoosh* away? They'd no longer be living rent-free in my head? These are dreams I can get behind. "Total sense." I grin.

Dr. Tracey says, "*This week's* plan, Maya, is for you to practice the window exercise three times. Deal?"

I give her a thumbs-up.

"Fantastic," Dr. Tracey says, pulling at her skirt again. "This time next week then."

The three of us get up from the couch in unison. Dad takes my hand as we walk out of the office. He has spots tonight, and Mama will help Baba with the store. But as we all hug goodbye and I get into Mama's car and Dad drives away in his own, I feel for the first time in a long time like we'll always be a family—no matter what.

CHAPTER 36

"She's unbelievable!" **Val hisses a week later as Ms.** Franklin assigns her to work with Barry for the second day in a row.

I've explained some about the tingles to Val and things I'm doing to get better. She's been great and has also taken it upon herself to tell people I left early the other day because of the flu. In typical Val fashion, it's a tale of great drama.

Today, as everyone starts getting into their groups, Ms. Franklin stops me. "Maya, it seems I forgot to put you with a partner. Would you like to choose a group?"

I look at Val's miserable face. My hands are clammy, and my heartbeat quickens, but I think I can do this. *Baby steps*, Dr. Tracey said this week.

"I'll work with Val and Barry," I say, and Val squeals.

I take a deep breath in, hold it, then slowly let it out. My fingers tighten around my pencil, and I walk to Barry and Val.

"Finally," Barry mutters when I plop down in a chair.

There's a *whoosh* in the distance, but it's not coming nearer.

"What are you so happy about?" Barry says, opening his laptop. "Researching this plane is going to take forever."

"I guess I don't mind planes today." I push my chair back to give us more room, place my pencil on the desk, and open my laptop. "Why don't I start?"

The next day, Mama runs out to deliver catering orders, and Baba calls me into the Gourmet kitchen. "Do you want to make syrniki with me?" she asks, arranging the ingredients for the cheese pancakes.

"Sure," I say, setting a container of raisins beside the eggs, packages of farmer's cheese, and flour.

We mix the ingredients together until they form a sticky paste, then dip our hands into the bowls and make balls with the dough.

"Don't forget to flatten each one, like so," Baba says, demonstrating.

I do, then add butter to the pan and wait for it to melt before plopping the batter in.

Babushka heaves a big sigh as she slowly walks back to the counter.

"You feeling all right?" I ask.

She winces and rubs her legs. "It's hard to stay on my feet as much as I used to, and the lines were never-ending yesterday."

I take off my gloves and bring her a chair. "Sit."

"There are still batches to make. Look at all the dough." She waves her hand over both our bowls.

"I can handle it," I say.

Babushka looks longingly at the chair and rubs her legs again.

I put my hand on her arm. "It doesn't make you weak."

She finally nods and sits down.

I put on new gloves to finish making the syrniki and feel her eyes on me the whole time.

"Thank you," she says, when I sit. She pats my hand and gives me a kiss.

When we come back to our own kitchen, I get her a heating pad and an extra chair to prop her legs. She hesitates only a second before letting me take care of her.

Baba places an arm over my shoulder and pulls me to her as we eat the pancakes.

Baby steps.

CHAPTER 37

That weekend, my feet trek through Ms. Banta's brown winter grass, and I run my fingers over the dusting of snow on her banister. The tingles started each time I thought about talking with her, but I decided if I can handle Barry, I can definitely talk with Ms. Banta.

Finger shaking, I ring the doorbell and wait. The sun is strong today, and I unbutton my coat.

The curtain lifts from the window, and for a second, I wonder if Ms. Banta will refuse to open the door. Just like I refused to call her back after the talent show.

The door is flung open, and Ms. Banta's warm smile helps ease the prickly feeling in my legs.

"Maya! It's so great to see you."

I clear my throat, trying to push my voice toward my lips. "You too."

"It's not bad out. You mind if we sit on the porch?"

I ease into the porch swing. Ms. Banta runs in for cookies and sits in a chair across from me when she returns. Her hands shake as she pushes the tin toward me. As happy as she seems to see me, it's obvious she's very nervous.

"My mom said it was okay for me to come see you?"

Ms. Banta takes a deep breath, holds it, then slowly lets it out. "Yes, I *want* to see you. It's just been a long time, and I know you're not happy with me."

I choose a vanilla-flavored cookie and carefully keep it in its paper wrapping as I take a bite. "I was upset right after the show, and I didn't know what to say. I'm sorry."

"No," she says. "I'm the one who's sorry."

She nibbles a cookie with a candy cherry in the center, eating around the middle.

"Ms. Franklin has been really good," I say. "She's even started cleaning the cushions."

Ms. Banta looks relieved. "I'm so happy to hear that." She pauses the nibbling and taps her cookie on her lips three times. "And Barry?"

I shrug. "My therapist gave me some ideas on dealing with him, so I'm trying them out."

"I'm sure that hasn't been easy." She absently runs a finger over the tin's lid.

"It's not. But I'm trying."

"You're brave," she says.

There's that word again. I shake my head no.

"You are," she says firmly. "Getting through the unknowns of each day is not easy. Coming here took a lot of courage, too."

I let the word *brave* roll around in my head. The tingles and *whoosh* are such a big part of me, they're all I've been able to see.

"You can come back," I say. "Even the board of education thought Mrs. Nelson's petition was stupid."

Her face falls. "I'm not ready to face people like that. I guess I'm not that brave yet."

I think about how Babushka finally put her feet up. How strength and bravery can come in so many different forms. How accepting help can be just as brave as facing your fears. "Maybe next year?"

Ms. Banta sighs. "That's my goal." She gives me a half-hearted smile. "I'm going to stay with my sister in Florida for a few weeks. Clear my head, enjoy the warm weather."

I finish my cookie and reach for a chocolate one. "That's a good plan."

"I'm looking into therapists, too." Her eyes look hopeful.

We sit a few more minutes in silence. Snow falls from the bare branches of Ms. Banta's oak tree.

"I heard you did great at the show. I'm sorry I missed it."

"I'm thinking of doing a kids' comedy showcase in New York, too. I'm not totally sure yet, but my dad and I have been crafting jokes."

Ms. Banta's eyes widen. "Really?"

I nod. "I really liked seeing how ideas can keep growing and changing, and making people laugh. Being onstage still makes me nervous, but I love creating the jokes, so I'm just focusing on that for now and we'll see."

And, who knows, with Dr. Tracey's help maybe I can combat the hot-hot-hot and get onstage, too. Whatever happens. There are no high stakes here.

Ms. Banta smiles at me again. "You've come a long way, Maya. You should feel proud." Then, she looks at her watch. "You probably need to help your mom and grandma?"

I don't, and Ms. Banta doesn't know if I do or not, but she's giving both of us an out. "Yeah, I should go."

"Don't be a stranger," she says, giving me a hug.

"You either."

As I walk down the porch steps, the air seems to grow colder. A car speeds by, its old engine roaring in the quiet late afternoon. My boots scrape against the asphalt, creating a new sound in my head. *Braaave, braaaave, braaaaave.*

I look back to Ms. Banta's house, surprised to see her in the window. When our eyes meet, she waves her arms and jumps up and down. I laugh and wave back.

A plane flies overhead, its *whoosh* loud and near. Its lights twinkle against the soon-to-be night sky. Thunder rumbles in the distance, and I pick up my pace and run faster and faster. I follow the lights of the plane and its booming *whoooosh*, making myself a part of the sound.

Composition

Maya's Favorite Recipes

100 Sheets • 200 Pages • Wide Ruled
9 3/4 x 7 1/2 in. • 24.7 x 19.0 cm

Babushka's Sour Cream Cake

INGREDIENTS:
1 cup sour cream
1 cup granulated sugar
1 cup all-purpose flour
1 egg
3/4 teaspoon baking soda
butter or margarine to grease a pan
matzoh meal to sprinkle on the greased pan

INSTRUCTIONS:
1. Preheat oven to 350 degrees.
2. Mix the sour cream, sugar, flour, egg, and baking soda together till it's a smooth consistency.
3. Use small amount of butter or margarine to grease a round cake pan. Then, sprinkle the pan with matzoh meal.
4. Pour mixture into greased pan.
5. Bake in the oven for 45 minutes.
6. Insert a toothpick in the center of the cake. If it comes out clean, the cake is ready.

Babushka's Cheese and Garlic Spread

INGREDIENTS:
10 ounces shredded cheese
4-5 tablespoons mayonnaise
6 fresh garlic cloves, grated

(My family loves garlic, but if the taste is too much, add more cheese as needed.)

INSTRUCTIONS:
1. Hand-mix all ingredients together until combined.
2. Spread on bread or crackers.

Babushka's Syrniki (Cheese Pancakes)

INGREDIENTS:

3 eggs
1 cup farmer's cheese, well drained (Don't confuse this with cottage cheese. Cottage cheese will make this dough watery, and the pancakes will fall apart.)
1 teaspoon vanilla extract (optional)
3 tablespoons granulated sugar
¼ teaspoon salt
5 tablespoons all-purpose flour, plus extra for dusting
oil for frying

INSTRUCTIONS:

1. In a large bowl, beat eggs. Whisk in farmer's cheese, vanilla, sugar, and salt, and mix until smooth. Add flour and mix well, until dough is thick and sticky.
2. Divide dough into 5 or 6 portions. Form into balls and coat with some flour. Flatten slightly to form into discs (syrniki).
3. Heat oil in skillet over medium-low heat. Add the syrniki; fry until browned, 5 minutes per side.
4. Serve with jam and/or sour cream.

ACKNOWLEDGMENTS

I give my utmost thanks to Kaitlyn Katsoupis and the Belcastro Agency for plucking me out of the slush pile and believing in me. Kaitlyn, I am beyond grateful to you for connecting with Maya, championing this book, being a sounding board, answering all my questions (and never saying I'm annoying), and always being my advocate. Your astute edits pushed Maya off the page. I'm SO lucky to have you. I am also very thankful to Alex Wolfe and the team at Penguin Workshop for seeing something in Maya and "getting" this book. Alex, I cannot thank you enough for your (many ☺) fantastic edits, keeping me in the loop of all things *Ain't It Funny*, and always making me feel like a partner in this project. I am also grateful for your WEALTH of stand-up knowledge that added so many layers to Maya's story. Thank you also to Mary Claire Cruz for designing a cover that captures the heart of this book and to Catarina Oliveira for vibrantly bringing the vision to life. A big thanks to my amazing friend Vinessa DiSousa for always being my cheerleader and not letting me give up on this journey. And, of course, thank you to Stu and Noah who had to put up with many nights of takeout and not enough time with me. I love you both so much, and you being proud of me means everything. And to Goosie, who supported me with his meows and purrs.

If you or someone you know is struggling with mental health, please know you do not have to suffer alone. The resources below provide helpful information.

American Academy of Pediatrics
www.aap.org/en/patient-care/mental-health-initiatives/mental-health-resources-for-families

National Alliance on Mental Illness
www.nami.org/Home

National Federation of Families
www.ffcmh.org